'Kiss me."

s Brenna's breath caught in her throat, her heart lurched a stop. Was there something to this honey-and-bees :ing? Maybe, with their chemistry leading them, they ould find common ground somehow.

avin continued in a low Texas drawl, "For some :ason, I find temperamental redheads fascinating all of sudden. Are you going to let me kiss you or not?"

I was waiting for you. Are you sure your lothario eputation is actually earned, because so far—"

His mouth covered hers mid-rant. His lips were warm, persuasive and sent a spark of desire shooting down her spine.

He cupped her jaw in his hand, angling her head to deepen the kiss, his tongue gliding against hers. She pressed her body against his, her hands clutching his soft cotton shirt as she fought to get closer.

Man, he felt amazing. She closed her eyes, shutting out her conscience, reminding her that she was kissing her opponent.

"I really don't need this complication in my life at the moment," he whispered hotly against her cheek.

"You're hopelessly arrogant," she returned, wrapping her arms around his neck and pressing against his firm chest.

"You're too serious." His lips moved over hers for another heated kiss.

"And

Dear Reader,

On February 17, 1864, the *H. L. Hunley* became the first submarine to sink an enemy vessel. Unfortunately, neither the ship nor the crew ever made it back to shore. For more than a hundred and thirty years, the fate of the *Hunley* was shrouded in mystery. Then in 1995, after a concerted effort by a team organized by author Clive Cussler, it was finally discovered four miles off the coast of Sullivan's Island, South Carolina. (One of the real-life islands that led to the creation of my own Palmer's Island.)

This story, along with information about the *CSS Alabama*, which raided merchant ships during the Civil War, inspired my own tale. Now, whether the *Alabama* had a pirate for a captain and booty of gold and gems on board is unlikely. But into the controversy of how to handle the recovery of my fictional ship, I've tossed Brenna McGary and captivating treasure hunter Gavin Fortune. These two are a volatile and electric combination, determined to protect history—and get their hands on each other as often as possible.

Thank you to all the readers who've been with my Palmer's Island novels from the beginning. I'm going to end here for now and move on to a new locale, but, rest assured, the gang on PI is enjoying their happily-ever-after—as well as running into mystery and adventure from time to time.

Happy reading!

Wendy Etherington

IRRESISTIBLE FORTUNE

BY
WENDY ETHERINGTON

Wendy Etherington was born and raised in the deep South—and she has the fried-chicken recipes and NASCAR ticket stubs to prove it. The author of more than twenty books, she writes full-time from her home in South Carolina, where she lives with her husband, two daughters and an energetic shih tzu named Cody. She can be reached via her website, www.wendyetherington.com.

To my sisters, Catherine Word and Laura Gurner, whose unconditional love and encouragement remind me that I come from good stock.

1

BRENNA MCGARY FLUNG OPEN the door of C's Styles and Spa.

Pausing only to wave at the receptionist, she stalked past two stylists and the nail tech's desk, zoning in on the shop's owner, Courtney.

Her friend and fellow historical society member, Sloan Kendrick, sat in Courtney's chair, her long blond hair encased in several dozen foil highlighting packets.

"Wait till you read the latest," Brenna said, waving the *Palmer's Island Herald*.

Sloan continued to flip through a fashion magazine. "That idiot reporter Jerry Mescle is way too wordy for me. Give us the bottom line."

"Gavin Fortune is part of the research team."

To Brenna's disgust, this announcement was met not by an echo of her own deeply held outrage, but by breathy sighs and rosy cheeks.

Courtney dropped her comb and snatched the paper from Brenna's hand. "Is there a picture?"

Two stylists left their clients to hover over Courtney's shoulder and take a peek. Even blissfully married Sloan leaned in.

Brenna rolled her eyes. Of course there was a picture. What was the fun of being a money-grubbing, morally vacant opportunist if you weren't also the hottest man on the planet?

And Gavin Fortune definitely fit that bill.

Even with that idiotic, had-to-be-made-up name.

Recently, a team of researchers from Miami had found a Civil War era ship a few miles off the coast of Palmer's Island and begun recovery procedures. *The Carolina* had cruised the waters and raided merchant vessels between the U.S. and the Caribbean from 1861 until the spring of 1863, when she and her crew arrived in Charleston Harbor to aid the Confederacy in the war effort.

Her seamen—cynics might call them privateers at best, pirates at worst—fought valiantly for the South for five months before the Union sank the ship on September 16. The location of the wreckage had become a fascinating legend to locals, due to the rumor of the ship's valuable cargo. The crew had supposedly been secretly carrying infamous pirate Captain James Cullen and his treasure chest of jewelry and gold coins.

Now, with glory-hound treasure hunter Gavin Fortune front and center, the Miami team had turned out to be exactly what Brenna and the other members of both the Charleston and Palmer's Island historical societies had feared most—a grave robber.

"Too bad the *Herald* can't afford to print in color anymore," Courtney commented, ruefully shaking her head of blazing red curls.

"Even in black and white, he's pretty dreamy," Sloan said as Courtney handed the paper to one of the other stylists, who wanted a closer look.

Brenna huffed in disgust. "Dreamy? Are you people insane? Gavin Fortune is the devil. The enemy. The scourge of historical societies the world over. The secretary of the Charleston group told me she started a website www.diefortunedie."

Brenna's friends stared at her.

Sloan angled her head. "Gee, Bren. We appreciate passion

in our members, but as long as you pay your dues, murder isn't part of the initiation ceremony."

"You need some highlights to calm you down," Courtney said, snagging her hand and leading her to the empty chair one station over.

Barely glancing at her strawberry-blond locks in the mirror, Brenna crossed her arms over her chest. "I told you guys those people were up to no good."

"We always figured they were more interested in the treasure than the historical aspects of the discovery." Sloan managed a small smile, even though Brenna knew she was just as worried. "That photo op looked more like an ad for swimwear than a serious scientific endeavor."

Brenna recalled the event, the recovery team posing on the marina's main pier with two bikini-clad girls holding up a gold plastic treasure chest, and her blood boiled all over again.

"But a lot of museums benefit from these kinds of finds," Sloan continued.

Brenna shook her head. "Not ones that rat Fortune is involved with. He swoops in, scrounges for valuables, then sells his treasures to the highest bidder. He doesn't care if the collection is bought as a whole or in a million pieces. We have to stop him."

"That's easier said than done." Courtney pulled Brenna's hair from its ponytail and brushed it out. "He's rich, famous and a media charmer."

Sloan bit her lip. "I'm not as concerned about him as an individual as I am about public opinion."

"They're fascinated," Brenna agreed.

"The mayor has visions of national exposure and Palmer's Island becoming another Kiawah-like resort destination," Sloan said.

Courtney glanced at her. "I thought he was stuck on getting a PGA-approved golf course."

Brenna sighed. "Somehow, I think he'd settled for a

hundred-plus-year-old treasure chest full of gold and priceless jewels."

Courtney picked up individual strands of Brenna's hair and
examined them closely. "I haven't touched this in a month.
How does it look better today than when I fixed it last?"

"Because her hair's perfect, as always," Sloan said.

Brenna shrugged. "Yeah, whatever." Her dad was an Irish
redhead, her mother a Southern-born bombshell blonde. She
got both—at least on her head. "Thanks," she added to her
friends, not wanting to seem completely churlish. Her hair
was one of her few features she actually liked. "But can we
stay on topic?"

"Hair or hot treasure hunters?" Courtney asked.

"*Amoral* treasure hunters," Brenna clarified.

"I vote you confront him."

At these abrupt words, Brenna stared at Sloan. "Me?"

"Sure." This time Sloan's grin was genuine. "I'm betting he's not the kind of guy who can resist an enraged Irish
pixie."

From anybody else, Brenna would have been wildly annoyed by this comparison. Her small stature was a serious
area of contention.

But she and Sloan had been friends since high school,
where she was head cheerleader and Brenna had been a champion gymnast. They'd fought together to be taken seriously as
athletes, surrounded by football, baseball and basketball play-
ers who were bigger, stronger and had their sports fully funded
by the school district. Brenna had even earned a scholarship
to the University of Florida and been an SEC champion on
floor exercise before a variety of knee injuries derailed her
career.

"I don't think that's a very good idea," she said finally
to Sloan's suggested confrontation. "I'm too angry to be
rational."

"You're always rational," Sloan pointed out. "You deal with

teenagers on a daily basis. If you can handle them, one amoral treasure hunter should be a relaxing vacation."

"I agree," Courtney said, her brown eyes sparking with enthusiasm. "You're the one who's done the research. You know all about Gavin Fortune and his tactics."

Brenna glanced from Courtney to Sloan. "Are you sure this isn't just a ploy to get a firsthand report of how hot this guy is?"

"Oh, no," Courtney assured her, though her face flushed too quickly to be convincing. "We're the historical society. We should have an official representative to let these guys know we're watching them."

Brenna swept her hand down her minuscule frame. "And you're sure I'm the one for the job?"

"Absolutely," Sloan said.

"You'd be better," Brenna insisted. The edge of her indignation was wearing off, rapidly replaced by suspicion. "You're the president of the society. Why me?"

"Because I have a pistol, and I know how to use it."

ON THE SHORT DRIVE TO THE marina, Brenna began to seriously question the plan.

Sure, Sloan was the former sheriff's daughter, and she did have a tendency to be impulsive and passionate, but she was their leader. Wasn't it her duty to handle the big problems?

Maybe Brenna had started the cause of watching the ship's excavation, but she had personal issues with the situation that had to be taken into account. And though she was upset, the whole "I'm too angry to be rational" thing had been a weak excuse. Mostly she was a talker, not a fighter.

She could easily intimidate high school kids with a glare, but confronting a man of Gavin Fortune's…well, breadth— given the tightness of his T-shirt in the newspaper picture— wasn't an area of strength.

Since Palmer's Island was an Atlantic Ocean barrier island near Charleston, South Carolina, just over three miles wide and five miles long, the trip from the centrally located hair salon to the marina at the tip—even with summer tourist season in full swing—took about three minutes. As she pulled off Beach Road, which ran the length of the island and allowed glimpses between the fabulous beach houses to the rolling sea sliding onto the sand, she searched the crowded parking lot for an empty space.

Tall palmetto trees, whose long green fronds swayed in the breeze, were flanked by their bushy shrub cousins and rows of sea oats. Puffy white clouds were the only things dotting the bright blue sky. Though the marina actually rested on the Intracoastal Waterway side of the island, at this end the land between the Atlantic and the waterway was only a couple hundred feet wide.

Her friend and lawyer, Carr Hamilton, lived on the opposite side of the street in a beautifully modern house on the point, and she cast a glance that way, wondering if he was home and if she should bring him along for this unpleasant confrontation with Gavin Fortune.

After shaking away that impulse and finally finding a spot at the end of the back row, she turned off the car and checked her reflection in the visor mirror. Small features, fair skin and "green as a shamrock" eyes, according to her father. She applied a little pink gloss to her lips, knowing no amount of makeup or surgery was ever going to turn her into a cover model.

She laid her hand over her cell phone sitting in the console. She should call Sloan and have her come meet her. Men fell at her feet—both before and since she'd married her darkly gorgeous husband.

The only male who consistently rubbed against Brenna lately was her prize Persian, Shakespeare Fuzzyboots.

With her hand wrapped around her phone, she caught a glimpse of the newspaper she'd tossed on the passenger's seat of her car. The confident smile and perfect teeth of Dr. Gavin Fortune flashed back at her.

Doctor? Ha!

He'd probably gotten an honorary degree from some university he'd donated a pile of cash to. His online bio had been vague, focusing on the high-profile treasures he'd found and profited from, not any actual qualifications he had for finding them.

With renewed determination, she stepped out of her car. She had a legitimate education. College had given her a teaching degree, specializing in literature, which she'd used in a variety of high schools throughout the South. She'd traveled through Europe, Asia and Greece. Sure, she lived on a small island, but she'd come home just two years ago, after her mother broke her hip playing tennis and needed her help.

The fact that she knew she was home to stay didn't make her unsophisticated. The island called to her sense of poetry, history and sheer appreciation of beauty. She wasn't hiding here. She certainly wasn't remembering how she'd found her last boyfriend in bed with the girl from Merry Maids.

After learning from the harbormaster that the research team was renting slip forty-two, she made her way down the pier, past a variety of speedboats, cabin cruisers and yachts.

She'd nearly reached her destination when it occurred to her that they might even now be at the wreck site scavenging for valuables. The vision of that atrocity had her quickening her pace.

With great relief, she saw a large cabin cruiser with the script *Miami Heat* bobbing next to the dock. Three men were standing on the bow of the boat. None of them was Gavin Fortune.

They noticed her approach, and the swarthy, Hispanic-looking one approached her with a smile. "Looking for Dr. Fortune?"

How had he known? "As a matter of fact, I am."

His grin widened. "I bet I could help."

"That's very kind of you to offer, but I really need to see him."

Shrugging, the man extended his hand to help her on board, then swept his arm in the direction of the boat's stern. "He's already turned away three today, señorita, but *buena suerte* to you."

Thanking him, Brenna rolled her shoulders. She'd take all the good luck she could get. But what three—

Her steps faltered. Three women. He'd already had others coming to find him. And she'd bet her entire collection of first-edition Yeatses that they hadn't come to call him out about his unethical research practices.

Were the women of Palmer's Island that hard up?

She found him leaning against the railing at the very back of the boat and focusing on a stack of papers held in his hand.

She was somewhat prepared for the wavy, sandy-brown hair, pulled into a short ponytail at the nape of his neck, but as she moved toward him, he lifted his head. His hazel eyes and the disarming dimples in his cheeks had a lot more impact live and in person than on her computer screen or in the newspaper.

But the circumstance that had her heart threatening to jump out of her chest was the fact that he was wearing a wet suit. At least from the waist down. The top half of him—all tan skin and lean muscle—was completely bare.

He sighed as she continued to stare at him mutely. "Let me guess, you're an amateur diver and you've always been fascinated by history."

She blinked at his deep voice, heavy on the Southern accent. Texas maybe. With reluctance, she raised her gaze to his face.

And all the moisture in her mouth dried instantly.

"Ah…no," she managed to say.

He straightened to his full height—a solid six-three—then strode toward her. "Look, honey, I've got a lot of work to do, so…" He stopped a few inches away, and she broke out in a sweat that had nothing to do with the blazing summer sun overhead. "How tall are you?"

By now, she should be used to the question, but he managed to startle her anyway. "Is that relevant?"

"You can't be over five feet."

She glanced down at her platform sandals, which added a good four inches to her height, and defiantly told the truth. "Four-eleven and three-quarters."

When she looked up again, his gaze was pinned to hers. "What do you do?"

"I'm a teacher."

"History? Social studies?"

Finally getting her bearings with his remarkable looks, she crossed her arms over her chest. "English literature, if you must know. Again, how is that relevant?"

"Oh, hell. Another Brontë groupie."

"I prefer Jane Austen."

If possible, he looked even more disappointed. "I was in a good mood today. I really was." He folded the papers in his hand, then walked past her toward the cabin area in the center of the boat.

Seeing little choice, Brenna followed him and didn't dare drop her gaze to see the back view of the skintight wet suit. "It's urgent that I speak with you, Mr. Fortune."

To her surprise, he didn't correct her about his title, fake as it might be. "It's Gavin, and I'm sure your cause is extremely important, but I have work to do." In the doorway of the cabin, he turned. "If you'll excuse me…"

Then he slid the door closed.

For several seconds, Brenna stood mutely on the other side of the glass barrier with her jaw hanging open. Only the prospect of humiliatingly facing Sloan and telling her she'd been aroused, intimidated, then turned away in less than three minutes by the same man she'd called the devil forced her to wrap her hand around the chrome handle and push the door aside.

Inside the cabin was a table bracketed on either side by black vinyl bench seats, a matching sofa on the opposite side of the boat, a kitchen area and a roomy cockpit. On the stern end was a closed door, presumably leading to a bedroom. Since Fortune was nowhere in sight, she assumed he'd gone into these private quarters.

She tapped on the door. "Mr. Fortune, I represent the Palmer's Island Historical Society, and it's imperative that I speak with you."

Silence.

Pressing her ear to the door, she thought she heard water running. Was he in the shower?

Fine. She could wait.

She sat on the sofa and mentally recited Robert Frost poems to keep her mind from wandering to the sure-to-be-enticing-and-distracting visual of Gavin Fortune standing naked under a spicket of water.

"The Road Not Taken," however, simply led her to stare in the direction of the closed bedroom door and wonder what lay beyond.

With monumental concentration, she reminded her libido she wasn't some creepy celebrity chaser. She was here with a serious purpose. She had justice, history and truth on her side.

He walked out in khaki shorts and nothing else.

She literally bowed her head. Was the man determined to derail her indignation?

To further annoy and embarrass her, he didn't even notice she was sitting on the sofa until after he'd retrieved a bottle of water from the fridge and turned to head back to the bedroom.

"How did you get in here?" he demanded, grinding to a halt.

Pleased she'd finally caught him off guard, she crossed her legs. "I opened the door."

"Then use it to go back out. I'm really very busy."

When he started toward the bedroom again, she lurched off the sofa directly into his path. The scent of sea air and woody citrus wafted from his skin, and she fought not to inhale too deeply. Droplets of water still clung to his wavy hair, which, released from its binding, hung nearly to his shoulders. If possible, the change made him even more attractive.

She cleared her throat. "Mr. Fortune, I represent the Palmer's Island Historical Society, and—"

"Why not the Society for the Defense of Boring Books? Or the Society for Unnecessary Exposition?"

Brenna narrowed her eyes, but she wasn't lowering herself to his insulting level.

Before she could so much as open her mouth, however, he rolled on. "Look, honey, I meet your type in every town I go to."

Brenna didn't think it was possible to be more insulted or enraged. Yet she was. "My type?"

"Sure. A crusader. No man, nothing better to do than harass hardworking people and write scathing letters to the local newspaper and city council. Do you have a cat?"

What did Shakes have to do with this?

"I'm here," she began in her sternest English teacher tone, "to discuss the graves you're disturbing, and the great tragedy you and your gang intend to profit from."

He laughed. He actually laughed. Again, annoyingly increasing his appeal. "My gang?"

"Yes, well…" That had been rather insulting, she supposed. After all, the Hispanic gentleman had been very gracious. "Your crew then."

"Who have five PhDs between the three of them. And you do realize this great tragedy happened nearly a hundred fifty years ago, right?"

"Doesn't matter."

"And this was a pirate ship, not the USS Benevolent Cruise Line?"

"Many so-called pirate ships were merely privateers who helped the war effort."

"For a price."

"Well, this ship aided the South, it was sunk by Yankees and I'm here to stand for the crew's noble sacrifice."

He cocked his head and studied her, as if truly looking at her for the first time. "Green eyes," he mused. "Fair skin, red hair, temper like a hurricane. Irish, by any chance?"

She raised her chin. "I'm a Southerner—eight generations worth, to be exact."

Very gently, he laid his finger in the dent in her chin. "Maybe so, but there's an Irish vixen some generation way back."

Desire shot into her stomach. She was pretty sure the same thing had happened to him, because the gold in his eyes suddenly deepened. His gaze fell to her lips and held. She curled her hand into a fist by her side to prevent the impulse to reach out and glide her fingers across his tanned chest to see if the muscles below felt as hard as they looked.

"Well, this is damn inconvenient, isn't it?" he asked in a low tone.

"I—" She stepped back, unsure if her embarrassing reaction to him or his acknowledgment of the chemistry between them worried her more. "We need to discuss the shipwreck."

"Fine." He moved around her and headed to the bedroom. "Let's go get a beer, and you can tell me all about your tragic cause."

She glanced at her watch. "It's three o'clock in the afternoon."

"So? I'll just throw on a T-shirt."

When he returned, he was wearing a gray T-shirt and had pulled his hair back with a leather thong no doubt also used by the pirates whose treasure he was so adept at finding.

Lost in thought, she dimly registered that he'd stopped in front of her.

His impressive chest rose, then fell as he sighed, and he,

too, checked the time. "It's not a complicated proposition. Beer, no beer?"

Spending any more time with this man than was absolutely necessary seemed unwise. And yet it had been so long since she'd looked at a man with anything approaching desire, she was reluctant to let the feeling die. She'd been sure her ex had killed all her sexual impulses as well as their future together.

"How about iced tea?" she finally suggested.

He curled his lip as he laid his hand at the small of her back and guided her to the door. "For you, maybe."

Outside, the wind had picked up, and Brenna flattened her hands against her sundress to keep it from flying up and giving Gavin Fortune and his crew an up-close-and-personal shot of her purple lace panties.

The blond-haired guy with wire-rimmed glasses smiled and nudged the Hispanic guy as they approached. "Pay up, Vasquez."

"Poker, boys?" Fortune asked. "I thought you were programming the ROV."

"No cards, amigo," the Hispanic man, presumably Vasquez, said with a quick glance at Brenna. "A different kind of wager."

"ROV?" she asked.

"Remotely Operated Vehicle," Vasquez said, pointing at a device sitting on a table near him.

It was clearly mechanical, with lots of interlocking metal parts and tubing. It looked heavy. And complicated.

And that was pretty much all she could grasp.

"Basically, an underwater robot," Fortune said, obviously sensing her confusion. "It allows us to take video and gather data without a human diver."

She nodded. He'd certainly been right about his crew's brains. "Oh."

"Pablo, this is—" Fortune stopped, regarding her with surprise. "What's your name, anyway?"

"Brenna," she said, sending him a reproachful look, realizing he'd never bothered to ask. "Brenna McGary," she said to Pablo, extending her hand.

"Pablo Vasquez," he returned. He indicated the blond man next to him. "This is Dennis Finmark. Over there is Jim Upton."

Brenna shook Dennis's hand and waved at Jim, a tall, thin, dark-haired guy who was wrapping a thick rope around a metal prong. They all seemed like nice, normal guys. Not minions of the devil at all.

She considered the implications of that as Fortune helped her off the boat, but it wasn't until they were walking down the pier that she finally understood the bet. "They wagered on whether or not I could pick you up."

"Excuse me?"

"You've already turned away three other women today."

"How do you know that?"

"Pablo told me." She halted, studying him from head to toe. "Does it ever get old, being infamous and irresistible?"

"Hell, no."

Ignoring his amused expression, she waggled her finger at him. "This isn't a pickup. It's a business discussion."

"Whatever you say, Miss McGary. It is *miss,* isn't it?"

"Yes, but how is that relevant?"

He resumed walking. "Just want to get your title correct."

No doubt that was a dig to her insistence on ignoring his doctorate. Well, if he wanted to change that, he'd have to show her his diploma first.

And the one from the University of Hot Bare Chests and Dimples didn't count.

When they reached the end of the pier, Fortune steered her right instead of continuing straight, which would have led them to The Night Heron, the marina bar. "The bar's this way," she said, pulling to a stop.

"Let's walk down the beach to Joe's."

"You know about Coconut Joe's?"

"Doesn't everybody?"

Given the fact that he hadn't bothered to put on shoes, she supposed the casual dress code of Joe's was more appropriate. She removed her platform wedges and moved down the stairs into the hot but soft crème-colored sand. "How long have you been on the island?"

"Two days."

"How long are you staying?"

"As long as it takes."

Okay, so not much of a talker. Not what she'd expected at all. He'd lost his cocky and careless expression and was watching the horizon.

Who was this guy?

They spoke little until they'd climbed the stairs from the beach to Joe's, which rose above the sand on wooden stilts. The tacky but charming decor, complete with the expected surfboards and fishing nets hanging on the walls, suited Palmer's Island's laid-back style perfectly. And the food was top-notch.

To escape the steaming summer heat, Fortune requested from the hostess that they sit inside with air-conditioning rather than on the screened deck. For some reason, Brenna had the feeling he would have preferred to be outside, but chose not to out of deference to her.

Clearly, the heat was affecting her brain.

She ordered sweet tea, and he stuck with beer. The waitress, named Tammy, gave the man across from Brenna a flirtatious smile and barely bothered to glance in her direction.

"Hey, aren't you the guy from the paper?" Tammy asked Fortune when she returned with their drinks. "You're some kind of cool scientist."

Fortune sent her a charming smile, including the dimples. "Maritime archaeologist."

Brenna nearly choked on her tea. *In what universe?*

The waitress's eyes widened. She leaned closer, giving him

and the entire back half of the restaurant an excellent view of her cleavage. "Wow. What's that?"

"I do research underwater. I've also studied history extensively."

Brenna barely resisted the urge to roll her eyes. *Is that what you earned your imaginary degree in?*

"I just love old stuff," the waitress said.

"No kidding? Old stuff is my specialty."

Brenna couldn't take it anymore. She took two large gulps of her tea and held up the nearly empty glass. "Could I get a refill, please?"

The waitress flashed her a resentful glare, but straightened and took the glass. "Weren't you my kid brother's science teacher last year?"

"English, actually."

"Don't worry, honey," Fortune said, leaning toward Brenna as Tammy stalked away. "There's plenty of me to go around."

2

"THIS IS A BUSINESS meeting."

There was something wildly arousing about that prissy mouth. Gavin couldn't remember the last time he'd enjoyed being scolded so much. "So why'd you chase off my opportunity for fun?"

She glowered at him. "You're a wretch."

"So?" But for the first time in a very long time he wished he didn't appear to be. "At least I have fun."

"I have fun."

"Oh, yeah? You and your cat get crazy on Friday nights and order anchovy pizza instead of just plain cheese?"

Her face turned bright red with her efforts to hold back her anger—the passion he wanted to see more than anything. "I don't like you very much."

"What a shame. I like you very much."

Leaning back, he sipped his beer and watched her coloring go from red to white in an instant. "Do you honestly think all it takes to get my attention is a set of big boobs and an interest in old stuff?"

"Priceless nineteenth century relics are glimpses into our past, how we lived, where we came from. They're representations of people who sacrificed for and dreamed of the world we now enjoy. They're reminders of our mistakes and successes, our tragedies and triumphs. They are not, nor should they ever be referred to as, *stuff.*"

There was the passion.

His body hardened, even as he cursed inwardly.

He'd cultivated his image carefully. Much of it might be a farce, but his popularity and daredevil reputation got him the important contracts. He couldn't risk exposure—even for a woman as exciting and challenging as Brenna McGary.

Sure, he'd grown tired of keeping up the pretense, and maybe some of the rumors attributed to him had gotten out of hand.

But he'd cast his lot a long time ago and didn't see how he could change his path now.

He had artifacts to protect, as no one else could. If lovely crusaders like Brenna had to hate him in order for him to accomplish the bigger goals, he'd have to suck it up and make the sacrifice. "Nice speech," he said, trying to seem impressed, but not too much. "I can see why the historical society values you."

"They certainly do. And that's why they sent me to confront you."

He spread his arms wide, giving her an easy target. "Confront away."

"We want the items recovered from the ship assembled into a single collection. We want the public and historical researchers to have an opportunity to view and study the artifacts. We want an effort made to contact descendants of the victims in the event anything with a personal monogram or family crest is recovered."

"So you want me to find the treasure, but you want to tell me how to do it?"

She looked annoyed by his assessment. "Not *how* in the technical sense. You clearly have qualified people and the right equipment. We simply want you to show some decorum. A little reverence for the task you're undertaking wouldn't be a crazy notion. And we don't want the artifacts auctioned off like livestock."

"I'm under contract with the descendants of the shipping company who owned *The Carolina*."

"Captain Cullen didn't own his ship?"

"If he did, he never registered the sale. It's possible he won the vessel in a card game, or even took it forcibly, but the last records we can find indicate the owner as the Sea Oats Shipping Company, so the artifacts I find belong to them."

"But you negotiate a certain percentage for yourself. And you can't tell me you report every find."

Gavin wished he could lash out at her accusation, but he frankly deserved it. He'd certainly been part of a team who'd committed that crime. "There are a lot of treasures down there, one of them possibly a chestful of gold and gems. There's no way the owners are going to plop it down in a glass museum case and charge five bucks a head to watch John Q. Smith walk by when they could make millions selling off the contents."

"So you haven't found the chest?"

"Not yet."

"But you think it's there."

He shrugged. "Legends generally have some basis in fact. Personally, I think we might find a chest, but a decoy. Pirates were clever and secretive when it came to their booty. Why would a successful one like Cullen blab about his?" Gavin reached into his shorts pocket and pulled out a bronze-colored coin, which he laid on the table in front of Brenna. "I did find this today."

"It's an Indian-head cent piece," she said, picking it up. "Circa 1860. These were issued by the U.S. Mint, not the Confederates."

"And *The Carolina* was known to raid Union merchant ships in the Caribbean."

Her fairy green eyes widened as they focused on him. "At least you've studied the history a bit."

"Why wouldn't—" He stopped. He could think of twenty reasons why reckless treasure hunter Gavin Fortune wouldn't be mistaken for a studious man. "I had some time on the flight up from Miami."

The waitress returned to see if Gavin wanted another beer, which he didn't. Brenna also declined any more tea. The meeting seemed to have come to an end.

Gavin was both glad and reluctant to part from her. He'd been reading some firsthand accounts of ship captains who'd encountered Cullen, and the latest batch was in French. Making any sense out of the various dialects, as well as the old-fashioned expressions, required serious focus.

Despite the fact that Gavin the Wretch would let her pay, he couldn't take the ruse that far. Teachers were shamefully underpaid, and he had plenty of cash to spare, after all.

But the unsettled feeling that had sunk into his gut since he'd heard her impassioned—and perfectly reasonable—list of requests about the recovery efforts refused to abate. Even as his bare feet sank into the hot sand while they walked back to the marina, the cold reality inside him remained.

He wanted to see much, much more of Brenna McGary, and he couldn't.

At least not in the way he'd like.

He was interested in her take on the differing accounts of Captain Cullen—as a heartless ravager of any and all ships in the Caribbean, or, in contrast, as a gracious seaman who always returned the passengers of the ships he overtook to a safe port. Was that a product of the Confederacy favoring him and the Union deriding him? Was it part of the pirate mystique? A combination of the two?

Even being raised in Texas, Gavin knew South Carolina was a whole different element of Southern culture. First to secede, they still flew the state flag with as much pride as the American one. With the first shots fired in the Civil War, they'd started out, and somehow remained, true rebels.

He'd love to hear her theories almost as much as he'd love to get her alone, aroused and naked.

Hey, he wasn't actually a wretch, but he was a man.

And it got old pretending to be stimulated by women who weren't interested in the things he was. Women who wanted to know how much things were worth, instead of what they meant.

"Why do you like me?" she asked suddenly.

Oh, boy. He fought against banality and pretty words. She was probably soft on Yeats, but a specific reference escaped him. "Why not?" he answered.

"Why not indeed?" She kept her face turned slightly away, so he couldn't see her eyes. "On the upside, I don't have big boobs or a tendency to call historical treasures *stuff.*"

"No. Everything about you is tiny." An instinctive smile broke across his face. "Except your mouth."

"It helps when attempting to control teenage boys. Do you want to know why I don't like you?"

He really wasn't sure he could take any more judgment from her, however justified. "My ponytail. I bet you hate long hair on men."

"No. The hair's…fine. It suits you."

"I'm not really big on shoes. Are you one of those women who uses shoe shopping to replace sex?"

"Definitely not."

"Then it must be because I'm an amoral, grave-robbing opportunist."

"That certainly plays a major part."

That wasn't *it?* He had faults besides his scoundrel image? Good grief. "What's the other part?"

"*Parts,* plural. I don't like people who think because I'm small I'm also weak."

Finally a question he could answer with absolute honesty. "I never, for one second, assumed you were weak."

"I'm so glad. I also don't like that you're all over the place."

"All over the place?" he repeated, trying to recall the last time a woman had caught him so off guard.

"At times you appear overindulgent and self-absorbed," she continued. "Then you say something intelligent, almost insightful. It's interesting."

He definitely couldn't have her thinking he was interesting. Her astuteness could ruin everything.

They'd reached the stairs leading from the beach to the pier, and she slipped on her shoes. "Thank you for your time. I'm sure we'll be seeing—"

"Sure you don't want to come back to my place for a while?"

"Your place?"

"Yeah. The boat." He inclined his head toward the marina. "I could tell the guys to take off for an hour or so."

"Gee, a whole hour?"

"Or so."

Her eyes frosted over. "No, thank you, Mr. Fortune."

"Call me Gavin."

"Not Dr. Fortune?"

"No way. That makes me sound like a comic book supervillain. How about Dr. Kensington?" He pursed his lips. "No, that makes me sound like an uptight English lit teacher."

"I neither have a doctorate nor am I uptight."

"But you sound like you do. I have two, and I don't."

"Two what?"

"Doctorate-level degrees."

"From where?"

"Cambridge and Princeton. Oh, and I got a masters in European history from Oxford. Just for fun."

Brenna burst out laughing. She giggled until tears leaked from her eyes. "Of course. Just for fun," she managed to say when she calmed enough to talk. "Thank you."

"For what?"

"For killing any attraction I might have been delusional enough to feel for you."

With that, she climbed the stairs and strolled down the wooden slats toward the parking lot.

He'd figured she wouldn't take either his real credentials or his fake tasteless proposition seriously, but he hadn't expected to be so disappointed in her reaction.

And the Yeats came back to him.

Here we will moor our lonely ship
And wander ever with woven hands,
Murmuring softly lip to lip,
Along the grass, along the sands,
Murmuring how far away are the unquiet lands.

IN THE LIBRARY TWO DAYS later, Brenna leaned against the front counter, no doubt distracting Sloan from her work. But everybody was working. Maybe she should get a summer job.

Of course, she was supposed to be focusing on *The Carolina* project for the historical society. And that thought led her right back to the place she'd sworn to quit going. "He's an insufferable egomaniac *and* an amoral, grave-robbing opportunist."

"You forgot gorgeous," Sloan said, never pausing as she tapped her fingertips on the computer keyboard.

"Looks don't figure into this."

"Sure they do. Helen said he's hotter than the Fourth of July sun."

Helen was another society member, who was also a business partner of Brenna's father. The two of them were the best real estate agents on the island.

Generally, Helen was a fine judge of man candy, and technically, she wasn't wrong in this case, though Brenna was loath to admit it.

She'd seethed for two days over her encounter with Dr. Gavin Fortune, whose mystery had only deepened. It took some digging, but with the help of the society's resident computer expert—a teenager named Penelope Waters—she hadn't found proof of advanced degrees, but a buried secret.

Fortune hadn't always been his name. He'd had it changed several years back. When Brenna had asked what his name had been before, she'd gotten a strange answer from Penelope.

"Nobody knows," she'd said. "The records were sealed by a federal court judge."

Beautiful, mysterious and possibly brilliant. What were the odds?

Too bad he was a complete ass.

"Helen also says he has a thing for you," Sloan continued.

"Well, he can keep his thing to himself."

"He seemed pretty disappointed to find Helen as the new historical society representative for his recovery project."

"I'm sure he was. He wouldn't dare pull the kind of crap on Helen he tried on me."

Sloan finally looked away from her computer screen. "What kind of crap...exactly?"

"He made fun of my cat, my temperament and my outspokenness. He derided a Brontë—he didn't mention which one—*and* Jane Austen, then made a clumsy pass. That's it."

"So you already told me. I still contend something else must have happened for him to run you off like that."

Brenna scowled. "He didn't run me off."

"Then why did you send Helen to deal with him?"

"Because I can't stand him."

Sloan's gaze probed hers. "You sure it's not because you like him too much?"

"In case you haven't noticed, Madame President, he's destroying the history of our island."

"I don't know about that."

"Mrs. Kendrick." A dark-haired girl of about ten walked up to the counter. "I'm supposed to find some books for my little brother. Can you help me?"

"Sure thing, sweetie," Sloan said, rounding the counter. "How old is he?"

"Four." The girl pursed her lips. "He can't really read yet, but he likes to pretend."

"I'm sure we can find something to help him on his way."

Brenna propped her chin on her fist as they walked away. Sloan was defending Fortune? What was that about?

Maybe Brenna was more sensitive than any of them about this particular project, but the rest of the society had to agree that Fortune and his crew weren't good for Palmer's Island. Even her father, who generally lived in the here and now unless a good spot of history helped him sell a property, was concerned about the fate of *The Carolina*. Before her parents had left on their month-long cruise, they'd encouraged Brenna to keep a close eye on the ship's recovery efforts.

She wondered what Grandmother would have thought about all of this.

Brenna had been raised on stories of Lucy McGary, her great-grandmother, who'd been a museum curator in Washington, D.C. In 1942, she'd been selected by the museum to transport several canvases of a well-known artist to London.

Unfortunately, the Germans had bombed their ship, convinced the vessel was transporting ammunition to the Allies. Her grandmother, along with fifty others, had been killed. The watertight safe of canvases had also met a watery grave.

Until 1992.

That year, the descendants of the artist convinced the ship's former owners to explore the wreck site and try to locate the lost paintings, which were now worth millions.

The excavation team, led by Dr. Dan Loff—who would later be famous for serving as mentor to Gavin Fortune—scavenged the sunken ship for treasure. When Brenna's family learned their relative's large, jeweled broach had been recovered, they flew to New York with pictures and proof of ownership, hoping to reclaim it.

Loff had already broken the setting apart and sold off the pearls and emeralds, one by one.

So if she was a little bitter toward vultures like Loff and Fortune, Brenna figured she had a right.

As Sloan returned to the desk, though, Brenna tried to set aside her personal prejudice and think logically. She wouldn't give a student a hard time just because his parents were rude. Maybe she'd wrongly stereotyped Fortune. She wasn't delusional enough to think good looks equated stupidity. Sloan didn't look like anybody's vision of a librarian, but she was brilliant at her job.

Though Fortune was still an ass.

There had been a fleeting moment when she'd thought she'd been wrong about him. When he talked about Captain Cullen, she'd sensed something in his tone. Excitement, maybe?

Then he'd admitted he'd simply read about it on the flight from Miami. He probably had a team of research assistants who culled together the facts he'd need to get through a press conference.

So what about the name change? Who had he been before? Why was it so important to protect that background? And why had he lied about his degrees? If he even had any?

No doubt being a brainiac didn't fit with his barefoot-with-a-ponytail, beer-drinking, hard-loving image.

"Did I mention I'm throwing a party tomorrow night at my house?" Sloan asked as she took her spot behind the counter.

Brenna struggled to drag her focus away from Gavin Fortune. "Party?"

"Yeah. Just the society, some of the supporters and the mayor. It'll be a social strategy meeting kind of thing."

"Sounds fun." And on a Friday night. *See, Dr. Fortune, I have plenty of fun.* She'd bet anchovy pizza wasn't on the menu, either. How had he known about that, anyway? "Can I do anything to help?"

"Yep." Sloan grinned, and for some reason Brenna didn't

like that smile one little bit. "Don't go crazy on Gavin Fortune and his team. They're the guests of honor."

"YOU'VE NEVER HEARD the expression about catching more flies with honey?"

Despite the fact that Sloan was digging her fingers into her arm, Brenna still wasn't leaving the kitchen. There was no way she was facing that man.

Guest of honor indeed.

"'The only way to have a friend is to be one,'" Brenna said in panic.

Sloan stopped trying to drag her to the doorway long enough to ask, "Yeats?"

"Emerson. I'm also rather fond of 'Thou shalt not betray your friends for the sake of hot maritime archeologists.'"

"Is that in Deuteronomy or Numbers?" Sloan asked sarcastically.

"The Gospel according to Brenna."

"I thought you said he wasn't hot."

Andrea Landry, another friend and Palmer's Island High alum, pushed open the door. "No luck?" she asked, her gaze skipping over Brenna and going to Sloan.

"She's stronger than she looks."

"Should I get the sheriff?" Andrea asked.

"Is that really necessary?"

Both women ignored her, but Brenna was encouraged by realizing the sheriff probably had better sense than to get in the middle of a chick fight—even if he was married to one of the participants.

True enough, the next person through the door was Sheriff Tyler Landry, who took one look at the fierce expressions on Brenna, Sloan and Andrea's faces and headed right back out again.

And he used to be a marine.

Not deterred in the least, her friends simply picked Brenna up and carried her through the doorway and down the hall.

Sometimes it really sucked being small.

After setting her down in the foyer, they nevertheless kept a tight hold on her arms as they inched into the front parlor. "Now remember," Sloan said, waving at the mayor as he walked by them with a loaded plate of food. "We're the bees, you're the honey and he's the fly we want to catch."

Brenna shifted her stare from one friend to the other. "You've got to be kidding."

"Not at all," Andrea said calmly.

Sloan nodded sagely. "Without the metaphors, he's a hot guy who likes hot girls."

"And you're a hot girl," Andrea added, in case Brenna didn't get the reference.

Brenna got it all right. But she didn't want to. She didn't like Gavin Fortune and didn't want to be anywhere near him.

A picture of his damp, shirtless body flashed before her eyes, and her stomach clenched. She *couldn't* be attracted to him.

It wasn't fair that the only man who'd gotten her motor running in the last two years had the morals and character of a starving hyena.

"Sloan has bigger boobs," Brenna returned, her heart racing with panic.

"The only hot, single girl," Andrea reminded her.

"I don't think he has too many standards in that area."

"But Aidan and Tyler do," Sloan said.

"Friends should come before husbands," Brenna said, as her gaze flitted around the room in search of Gavin Fortune. She finally spotted him in the corner of the parlor, surrounded by—who else—a group of smiling women. And one of them happened to be Penelope Waters.

They couldn't let him get his hands on an innocent like Penelope.

But why did she have to be the one to sail to the rescue? "Helen and Courtney are single."

"But he's interested in you," Sloan said.

Brenna's eyes widened. "So you want me to seduce him into meeting our demands?"

"I don't know if you need to go that far…." Andrea began.

Sloan grinned. "But it couldn't hurt."

"We wouldn't want Brenna to compromise herself." Uncertainty slid across Andrea's face, and Brenna felt a surge of hope.

"Who's talking about compromise?" Sloan argued. "I bet he's great in bed."

"His body certainly seems fit," Andrea said slowly. "And he doesn't lack for confidence."

Sloan sent Andrea a knowing look. "Seducing the man of your dreams worked for you."

"Hellooo? Guys?" Brenna's tone rose in alarm as she dug in her heels and brought them all to a standstill. They really were going to throw her at the wolf's feet. "Remember me? Don't you think I should have some say in this plot of yours?"

"No," Sloan said at once. "You're too emotionally involved."

"And you're the one who was so passionate about this project," Andrea added. "Don't you want to save *The Carolina* and her treasure?"

That was hitting below the belt. "Gavin Fortune is not the man of my dreams!"

"You wound me deeply with your barbs, fair Irish queen."

Brenna's gaze shot to the circle of women where Gavin had been standing only moments before. The women were there, but no Gavin.

He was standing right behind her.

She whirled, and her sudden movement caused Sloan and Andrea to drop her arms. She was finally free, and she longed to run, but she found herself rooted to the spot, caught by the laughing hazel eyes of Gavin Fortune.

How much had he heard?

"I'm great in bed, by the way." His smile turned wickedly inviting. "I'm an avid swimmer, and you know, it's all about stamina."

And despite comments like that one, her body leaned toward him. It was humiliating.

Hadn't she laughed at him the last time she'd seen him? Hadn't she vowed he'd killed her attraction with his ridiculous lies about his credentials?

But *were* they lies?

When she remained furiously mute, Sloan and Andrea introduced themselves. The three of them exchanged pleasant chatting while Brenna's blood pressure rose, and she fought to remind her libido that she wasn't hard up enough to remotely consider throwing herself at her enemy. Even to protect priceless treasures. Even though the fact that he was within touching distance made her fingers tingle.

Along with other, more intimate body parts.

"Still too intimidated to talk to me?" Gavin asked her.

Brenna glared at him. "Not hardly."

"You found out I'm smarter than you, and sent over your real estate friend rather than deal with me."

"What smarts?" Brenna returned through clenched teeth. "You lied about those degrees."

"Did I?" His hazel eyes danced. "You don't believe I know what I'm doing?"

No way was she going there. "I'm too busy to deal with you."

"What a shame." He leaned close enough that she could smell his enticing cologne and see the telltale gold flecks in his eyes. "I'd really like you to come back."

She swallowed hard. "You would?"

"Sure." He straightened, his expression smug. "If you don't, Helen's going to wind up selling me half the island."

Brenna felt heat climb up her neck. "With all your ill-gotten gains, you could certainly afford it."

"You bet I can," he returned with equal resentfulness. "But

I'm sure one sage quote from you via some boring English poet would change my life, make me see the error of my ways and get me to donate all my profits to some moldy museum."

"Wow," Andrea said, her tone awed. "Helen was right about you two."

"You'd be smokin' together," Sloan agreed.

Brenna glared at her friends.

Andrea was an art historian and expert appraiser. Why wasn't *she* the one forced to deal with the arrogant treasure hunter? Sloan was president of the historical society. She should have to listen to his come-ons and stubbornness.

Then, like an angel sent from heaven, she saw her salvation.

Another high school friend, Carr Hamilton, had started dating a tough-minded, always-armed FBI agent in the spring. Though gooey in love with Carr, her live-in boyfriend, Malina Blair was intimidating as hell to everybody else.

She was perfect.

Without a glance to those around her, Brenna darted to Malina's side and rudely interrupted the welcome kiss between her and Carr.

"How do you feel about murder-for-hire?" she asked, relieved to note Malina's sidearm was indeed in its holster.

Malina's turquoise eyes widened, then turned speculative. "Depends on who I'm killing." She paused, angling her head. "I assume I'm the killer in this scenario?"

Brenna grabbed her arm and tugged her toward the group surrounding Gavin Fortune. "Definitely."

3

BRENNA STOOD ON Sloan's back deck, her neck craned as she stared up at the stars.

The sticky summer heat lingered in the air, and though she'd be more comfortable inside with the air-conditioning, the party had long since lost its luster. If it ever had any.

She wished she could be launched to that star, the third from the right. It looked peaceful and welcoming.

And galaxies away from Gavin Fortune.

Clearly, there was no justice on this planet anymore. Even Malina was charmed by him. The kick-ass agent had patted Brenna's shoulder and pronounced, "It's not a crime to be a flirt."

Brenna was on her own in her resentment and suspicion.

Hearing the back door open, then close, she didn't have to turn to know who'd joined her on the deck.

And she wasn't so far gone into melancholy that she didn't realize she needed to draw first blood. "I don't like you."

He leaned against the railing beside her. "And all your friends do. That must really suck."

"You have no idea."

"Maybe you're trying too hard not to like me?"

Eyes wide, she turned her head and stared at his profile. "Are you delusional?"

Not seeming at all offended, he angled his head in consideration. "I don't think so, but then if I were, how would I know?"

"Is it any wonder I want to run in the opposite direction every time I see you?"

He leaned toward her. "Face it, you have the hots for me."

"Sure I do," she returned sarcastically, hoping he couldn't hear her heart rate pick up speed. Propping her forearm on the deck railing, she forced herself to hold his gaze and move closer, until their faces were mere inches apart. "Probably because of all those compliments about me and everything I care about."

"I'm a scientist," he said, his gaze flicking to her lips. "I'm required by law to hate literature."

"You don't seem like much of a rule follower. Do you really hate all the classics? Or is it just not cool to read?"

"Dickens had his moments, and I do like Yeats, but I'm more of a modernist when it comes to pleasure reading."

He really did have a gorgeous face. "Well, I'd appreciate it if you wouldn't put down the things I like."

"And I'd appreciate it if you wouldn't judge me without even knowing me."

When he licked his lips, she bit back a groan. "I'll do my best."

"Tell you what, if I keep my derogatory comments about English poets and long-winded nineteenth century literature to a minimum, will you participate in an experiment?"

"What experiment?"

"Kiss me."

As her breath caught in her throat, her heart lurched to a stop. Were Sloan and Andrea right? Was she jumping to conclusions? Would she and Gavin be great together? Was there something to this honey and bees thing? Maybe, with their chemistry leading them, they could find common ground somehow.

He continued in a low Texas drawl, "I haven't stopped thinkin' about you since you stormed off the other day."

She coughed to clear her throat. "You've been on my mind quite a bit, as well."

His perfect teeth flashed in a smile. "Anything you want to mention, between the cuss words and name calling, that is?"

"Your degrees are imaginary."

"Are they?" He seemed surprised.

"I had the historical society's resident computer expert do a little research. She discovered your name change, by the way. Care to elaborate?"

"Fortune is descriptive—and sexy, don't you think?"

That wasn't an answer. A confirmation. Or a denial. *Hmm...* "It's something, all right. I saw you talking to her earlier."

"Who?"

"My computer expert—Penelope Waters." Brenna narrowed her eyes. "Who you need to take off your radar instantly."

"I don't fool around with kids."

"Or big-breasted waitresses."

"For some reason, I find temperamental redheads fascinating all of a sudden. Are you going to let me kiss you or not?"

"I was waiting for you. Are you sure your lothario reputation is actually earned? Because so far—"

His mouth covered hers midrant. His lips were warm, persuasive, tasting appealingly of whiskey and sent a spark of desire shooting down her spine.

He cupped her jaw in his hand, angling her head to deepen the kiss, his tongue gliding against hers. She pressed her body to his, her hands clutching his soft cotton shirt as she fought to get closer.

Man, he felt amazing. She closed her eyes, shutting out her conscience, which was trying to remind her that she was kissing her opponent.

"I really don't need this complication in my life at the moment," he whispered hotly against her cheek.

"You're hopelessly arrogant," she returned, wrapping her arms around his neck and pressing her aching breasts against his firm chest.

"You're too serious." His lips moved over hers for another heated kiss. "And you could be a lot quieter."

She was perfectly happy with the method he used to silence her.

He had a great mouth, and the hunger that twisted low in her belly spread and intensified. As his hands slid down her back to cup her butt and tug her against his erection, she moaned.

The heat that had flared briefly between them a few days ago raged into a white-hot fire, leaving her body throbbing, and incinerating every vow she'd made about keeping her distance from this man.

He not only had her motor revving, it was on the verge of blowing. Yet she didn't do one-night stands. And she couldn't imagine anything with Gavin Fortune lasting beyond one night.

They were adversaries at best, stone-cold enemies at worst.

This same thought seemed to occur to him at the exact second it did her, since they both jumped back simultaneously.

"We can't do this," he said, his breathing harsh and choppy as he stared in disbelief at her.

"You started it," she snapped, annoyed that she wanted nothing more than to be back in his arms.

"Me? You were all over me."

"Excuse me, Mr. Delusional. You were the one who proposed the experiment."

"Which was a complete failure. I don't want you in the least."

"Me, either." Every cell in her body tingled, calling her a liar. "I'll have no problem doing my duty by the historical society and checking up on every move you and your crew makes."

He crossed his arms over his chest and attempted to look aggravated, even though she could see the desire lingering in his eyes as his gaze focused on her lips. "It's summer. Can't you set aside the overbearing teacher impulses until September?"

"Unfortunately for you, no."

"Fine."

"Good."

Breath heaving, they glared at each other. In the next instant, they were plastered together.

GAVIN LEANED BACK in his deck chair on board the *Heat* and closed his eyes against the glaring sun overhead. "I'm in serious trouble, amigo."

Pablo, lounging in his own chair, needed no clarification on the cause of Gavin's problem. "She's a looker. Could use a tan, though." When Gavin glanced at him, he peeked over his sunglasses, his eyes lecherous. "Why don't you invite her to sunbathe on deck tomorrow? I'll watch over her while you pick through all that debris at the wreck site."

"That's a great plan," Gavin said in mock admiration. "Why didn't I think of that?"

"No idea. You're the one who's supposed to be brilliant."

"Sure I am. She can hardly stand the sight of me, so I'll just call her up, invite her over and ask her to strip down to her bikini while we all drool over her."

"I'll be drooling. You'll be diving."

"Even better."

"It is. She likes me better than you."

"Oh, no, she doesn't. You're guilty by association. She thinks you're part of my *gang*."

"I wouldn't be if you'd tell her you're not a jerk."

Gavin shook his head. "I can't risk it." He paused, feeling

the weight of his lies more substantially than ever. "Besides, she'd hardly believe me now."

With a sigh, Pablo sat up. "Keeping up your hotshot image gets you a lot of play, and our team a lot of press. Your agent called earlier, by the way. He wants to talk to you about a cameo in the next Dr. McFearsome movie."

"Dr. McFearsome?"

"He's the suave archeologist who's obsessed with Egyptian culture, Tai Chi and hot blondes."

Gavin winced. "Charming."

"Could be fun."

"I don't see how."

After a tick of silence, Pablo conceded, "If you're miserable with your image then dump it. You don't have to compete with Dan Loff anymore."

Gavin curled his hand into a fist. "Loff doesn't have anything to do with this."

"Sure he does." Pablo swatted his shoulder and stood. "Way too much."

As Pablo walked toward the cooler, Gavin reflected that though Loff had been the catalyst and motivation for much of his professional life, Gavin himself had made the choices that had brought him to the crossroads he now faced.

He'd wanted the spotlight, and he'd gotten it. He could hardly complain about the results at this stage of the game.

"You want a beer?" Pablo asked, holding up a bottle.

"Yeah." As his friend passed one over, Gavin wondered, "What's for dinner?"

"Who am I, the little woman? Did you catch something today besides the blues?"

Gavin unscrewed the top of his beer bottle and took a long sip. "No. I got distracted by the buttons."

"Brass?" Pablo asked as he settled back in his chair.

"Yeah, and with an eagle emblem. By 1863 the metal was hard to come by for the South, so it's a pretty good find."

"Could be off a Union uniform. The pirates had better gear than either side."

"True."

They drank in silence for a few minutes. Gavin watched a plane cruise by with a banner that read, Cal's All-You-Can-Eat Seafood. 5-9 Daily Specials.

The Islanders would hate that. Anything interrupting the natural peace of their sandy paradise was met with derision or legal action. Even his expedition was likely to be tolerated more than planes, helicopters, motorcycles or an overabundance of Jet Skis.

Silence was golden.

Since he spent a great deal of his time in the dark and quiet, underwater, he could appreciate the sentiment.

He definitely liked kissing Brenna McGary into silence.

On another gulp of beer, he wished, futilely, for a moment's peace from thoughts of that woman.

The woman he wanted beyond all reason. The one who tempted him to throw away the caution that—secretly, anyway—guided his every move.

If Sloan Kendrick hadn't walked onto the deck and interrupted their make-out session, Brenna would have spent last night in his bed.

Which would have been a very bad move.

His body throbbed in protest.

She was determined to demonize him to the mayor, city council and the historical society. Even the damn sheriff had given him a stern look before Gavin had revealed—truthfully, for once—that he'd been raised in Texas and had a serious love for college football.

Charming this place was becoming a serious task. Over the last few years he'd taken for granted that particular aspect of his job.

If Brenna incited picketing or negative media reports, he'd be in a world of hot water with the owners of *The Carolina,* who needed quick cash for their treasure. As seemed to be the norm, it was up to him to care about the artifacts he found.

Him and Brenna.

She'd appreciate the irony if he ever had any intention of telling her the truth about himself.

"What graves did you dig up today, boys?" a familiar voice called from the direction of the pier.

Gavin's pulse shot up. "Oh, hell."

"It's that attitude that's making you so hateable." Pablo leaped off his chair. "I, on the other hand, would be glad to take care of our Irish pixie."

"Our—" Gavin rolled to his side and gained his feet, rushing after his buddy. "She's my problem."

As they moved forward, Pablo nudged him aside. "A woman should be revered and cherished. You don't deserve her."

Though part of him realized Pablo was simply messing with him, Gavin still found his blood boiling. No other man was coming within ten miles of *his* Irish pixie until they'd settled this conflict/passion/craziness between them. "Hey, pal, I saw her first."

"No, you didn't."

They arrived on the bow just in time to see Brenna and Penelope—the society's teenaged computer guru—walking down the gangplank.

Carrying a cooler, Brenna wore white Bermuda shorts and a bright green halter top. The high-heeled wedge sandals she used to overcome her issues with her stature were also present. And though he didn't think her size diminished either her power or her beauty, he had to admit they did amazing things for her legs.

Since Pablo seemed determined to best him in the gentleman's game, he let his friend take the cooler, then Brenna's hand, and assist her to the deck, while Gavin did the same for Penelope.

The nineteen-year-old had lovely and curious brown eyes, which, if Gavin had been a decade younger and never encountered the fiery Brenna, would have intrigued him endlessly. "My technical expert is already gone for the day, Penelope, but if you'll let me know when you want to come back, I'll set up a meeting for you. He'd be glad to show you the Microseaomitter."

Behind her glasses, her eyes widened. "Really?"

"Absolut—"

"Don't let him sway you, Penelope," Brenna interrupted, her green eyes fiercely fixed on his. "No telling how many treasures he's absconded with today."

"I thought we agreed you wouldn't judge," Gavin said.

"I thought we agreed your radar wouldn't include certain innocents," Brenna countered.

"My sensors are otherwise occupied at the moment."

Penelope, as intelligent as she was, certainly sensed the tension between him and Brenna. "He's just being kind, Miss McGary. We talked about the Microseaomitter at the party last night."

"That's fine, but I told Sister Mary Katherine I'd be responsible for you."

"I'm an orphan," Penelope said to Gavin and Pablo. "My parents were killed in a car accident when I was little, and the Sisters raised me. However..." She narrowed her eyes in Brenna's direction. "I'm nineteen now and about to start my sophomore year at the College of Charleston."

Brenna offered the group an uncertain smile—like a parent, uncomfortable with how to publicly handle an outspoken child. "And everyone's so proud of you."

Not backing down in the least, Penelope crossed her arms over her chest. "I can take care of myself."

"I know," Brenna said, looking a bit panicked.

Since Brenna excelled at giving him a hard time as well, Gavin was firmly on the teen's side in this standoff.

"How am I ever going to be responsible if you guys never let me out of your sight?" Penelope returned.

"I don't really have control of—" Brenna began.

"I'm a legal adult," Penelope said forcefully. "I have control of my own life. I have my own apartment and pay my bills."

Brenna grabbed the teen's hands. "I'm so sorry. I truly didn't mean to give you a hard time about coming here. I just…" She trailed off as her gaze found Gavin's again. "Got carried away."

Even as Gavin understood this message was for him and the night before, Penelope's face turned bright red. She seemed to realize there were people present besides her and Brenna. "Oh, my goodness."

Pablo, firmly in gentleman mode, patted her on the back. "It's okay, señorita. Asserting your independence is a time-honored tradition on this boat."

"It's probably the sea air," Gavin added.

"Or the sun," Brenna offered.

"I grew up here!" Penelope wailed as she accepted the towel Pablo handed her and dabbed her tears. "I'm used to the sea and the sun."

"Then it's gotta be romance," Gavin said, sending a commensurate glance in Brenna's direction. "Only intense attraction can make a lovely, intelligent woman—or irresistibly brilliant man—irrational and despondent."

Penelope bowed her head. "I don't have a boyfriend."

After a significant pause, Pablo said, "Don't worry, honey. You will."

Behind Penelope's back, Brenna gestured to Gavin, who joined her a few feet away. "Fix this," she whispered.

"How?" Immediately, he inhaled the faintly floral aroma that clung to her skin and made all the nerve endings in his body stand at attention. "I'm not allowed to even touch her."

Brenna scowled. "You can console without touching."

"How?" he repeated.

"Be verbally supportive."

The woman was going to literally drive him over the edge. He couldn't work, he couldn't think and now he couldn't relax without her interference. Without her…presence. Her scent and the lure of stroking her velvety skin permeated every breath he took.

"You're the talker," he retorted. "*You* be verbally support-ive. Pretty much all I've thought about since you stepped onto my boat is how to get you naked."

Her eyes turned smoky, then cleared. "That's not help-ful."

"Sorry."

"I even brought a peace offering." She pointed to the cooler at Pablo's feet. "I've got flounder and salad on ice."

"For what?"

"Dinner."

He pictured candlelight, moonlight, the cozy confines of his cabin. Wine, both of them talking as little as possible. The combination could lead to anything.

Possibly even nakedness.

Though he'd just assured himself it was smart of them to have escaped last night without any more physicality than the vertical make-out session, his resistance when faced with her was crumbling like the wooden frame of the ship she was so determined to defend.

Being near Brenna wasn't wise, but he didn't seem to have a choice anymore. She was determined to keep a close eye on him, and there was no way he could continue to resist her for long.

Surrender could be pleasurable, right?

"You brought dinner for us?" he asked, trying to focus on the present rather than the optimistic future.

"Well, for everybody."

And the bubble of hope burst.

Pablo and Penelope were on board. And the reason Brenna had brought her young friend was suddenly apparent. "You need a chaperone to be in the same room with me?"

"Yes. I'm in charge of supervising you and your crew for the historical society, if you remember. Though consoling Penelope seems to be a greater priority at the moment."

Gavin glanced at the teen, who had her head on his friend's shoulder. "Pablo's got it."

Brenna looked annoyed. "Your sensitivity needs a lot of work."

"I'm not the one smothering her," he said smugly.

"Ahoy!" called an unfamiliar male voice.

"What new hell is this?" Gavin wondered, directing his attention to the gangway.

A cop was boarding the *Heat*. Young, probably early twenties, he wore a khaki-colored uniform on his tall, lanky frame. His spiky blond hair stood up in stylish tufts Gavin had seen on various teen pop stars, but his eyes were light blue and serious, as if they'd aged out of proportion to the rest of him.

This wasn't the sheriff, he knew, since he'd met Tyler Landry at the party the night before. A deputy, maybe?

"Miss McGary," the officer said with a nod as he approached them.

Brenna made brief introductions all around, and Gavin learned the man was Finn Hastings, a deputy, as well as the sheriff's brother-in-law.

"I just came by to check on you," he said to Gavin. "There are a few people in town not happy to have you around. I wanted to make sure they weren't giving you a hard time."

Somehow, he managed to say this with a serious expression and not glancing once at Brenna.

But then Brenna wasn't paying much attention to the deputy. She was staring at Penelope, who, in turn, had her wide-eyed gaze fixed on Finn, who was gaping right back.

Well, well. The time-honored tradition to fixing teenage woes had apparently not changed since Gavin was that age. Just plop a hot guy and girl next to one another, and the sun shone from behind the clouds.

"We're fine," Gavin assured Deputy Hastings. "Brenna even brought us dinner. Flounder, I believe."

Finn tore his attention away from Penelope and lifted his eyebrows. "Did she?"

"The seafood stand in the marina parking lot," Brenna said, and Gavin noticed her eyes narrow in speculation while gazing at the youngsters.

Ah, good. They were on the same page.

Get the kids together, then Gavin could handle getting rid of Pablo, then he and Brenna could be alone.

It was possible, of course, that Brenna was only thinking of consoling Penelope, and not of spending the evening staring across the table at him, but he was betting he could negotiate that little hitch.

"Are you sure you brought enough for five?" Gavin asked her. "I could go get more." Cooperation and generosity were the ways to her heart, after all.

But he was counting on the teens not being interested in hanging out with the adults.

"Sorry, I can't stay," Finn said.

Penelope nodded, though her gaze remained riveted to Finn. "I should really get back home."

"I could give you a ride," Finn offered. "I was on my way home, too."

Penelope's mouth parted in a shy smile. "That would be nice. Thank you."

It was great to be right.

"I'm not sure—" Brenna began, but Gavin cut her off by laying his hand at the lower part of her back.

"Escorted safely to her door by the police," he said. "How could the good Sisters be more pleased by that level of chaperoning?"

"I agree," Pablo said, with a definitive nod that Gavin would make sure he received a raise for. "And there should be plenty of food, because I have a dinner engagement at the marina bar."

A really big raise.

Within two minutes, the trio was walking down the dock away from the boat, leaving Brenna and Gavin blissfully alone in the shadow of the setting sun.

"That happened fast," she said, turning to him in surprise.

"Didn't it?" He smiled. Oh, yeah, surrender was chock-full of delight. "But who are we to stand in the way of young love?"

4

"THE FLOUNDER'S WONDERFUL," Brenna said from across the candlelit table.

"Thank you." Gavin toasted her with his wineglass. "Cooking skills are mandatory for a bachelor who spends a lot of time alone on the water."

She leaned back in the bench seat and glanced around the cozy cabin. Moonlight streamed through the windows and waves slapped gently against the boat's hull. This wasn't what she'd expected from her peace offering.

This was way too intimate. Romantic. Tempting.

She'd counted on Penelope to give the dinner a neutral, even academic tone. They were going to fry fish and talk about history. Low lights, delicately grilled flounder and fruit-infused wine weren't on the original menu.

And what had happened between Finn and Penelope, anyway?

Though, frankly, she did understand the mechanics of what had happened. It was happening to her, too, after all. Hormones. Pheromones. Uncontrollable chemical reactions.

But the ex-con and the orphan raised by nuns?

Now, *that* was an odd combination.

Then again, romance could be a strange…

"Wait." Her gaze zipped to Gavin. "Alone? When are you ever alone?"

"I like solitude. The crew rented condos on shore, so I—" He stopped, then sipped his wine as if giving himself time to gather his thoughts. "Though I'm only by myself when I'm not hooking up with a babe from the beach."

Brenna carefully set her wineglass on the table. "Naturally."

Still, there was something odd about his abrupt bragging. Was it true or just talk? He was gorgeous and successful enough to have anybody he wanted, but was a cute girl in a bikini his only requirement?

He'd sworn he wasn't interested in the waitress the other night. And, come to think of it, why wasn't he?

The flirty woman should have been a fantasy incarnate for Dr. Lothario—obvious, easy and temporary.

What was his deal?

"Today, however," he began, his tone quiet, "I've thought a lot about you."

"So you were ticked off all day?"

He smiled—not the debauched one, but the one that made her breath catch. The one she wished was genuine. "At times." His gaze moved to hers. "We're really very…different. And yet I like debating with you. I like your strength and determination. I especially liked kissing you."

Her lips tingled as if he'd touched them. "Didn't we agree last night was an impulsive mistake?"

"We did. I didn't say it was smart to like kissing you."

"I know why I don't like having the hots for you. Why don't you like—"

"Last night you said I was delusional for thinking you had the hots for me."

The man never let anything go. "I think after the impulsive and unwise make-out session last night, we can stipulate we have the hots for each other."

He forked up another bite of fish. "Agreed."

"So why aren't you happy about our attraction? Given your reputation, you don't seem overly picky about your romantic liaisons."

"Romantic liaisons," he repeated, shaking his head. "That description is exactly why our chemistry is inconvenient. I'll be here a few weeks, a month at the most. My distractions from work are short-lived, and I never get involved with anyone exclusively. You seem like the long-term, exclusive type."

"I am." And the fact that he recognized those qualities about her, and was trying to avoid her as a result, was practically chivalrous. So all the more confusing. "However, my body and my brain seem to be disconnected right now."

"I know the feeling."

Certain the frustrated heat in his eyes was reflected in her own, she scooted to the end of the booth. "I should go."

He grabbed her wrist. "Don't."

Her pulse pounded at the point of contact. Swallowing hard, she closed her eyes. The desire, unfortunately, didn't vanish.

She wanted him beyond reason or practicality. And she sure as hell didn't care about fleeting—in fact, temporary was best.

As long as he could temporarily satisfy the needy ache that had settled deep inside her, ruling over every thought and action, he could then leave the island and take all temptation with him.

"At least finish your dinner," he said, releasing her. "You were kind to bring it."

She moved back in front of her plate and took a gulp of wine. Her heart was pounding irrationally hard. "It was meant to help us get along as professionals."

"But we probably shouldn't get along."

"Good point." Again, she sipped from her glass. "Why don't we talk about something we don't agree on?"

"That's pretty much everything."

"Great. Keep your mouth moving."

His pupils dilated.

"Talking," she clarified, feeling a rush of panic. He was so close. Too close. "Keep talking."

"Fine. When we dove today, I found some—"

"Have I ever told you about my grandmother?" She broke in, realizing this was a topic that was sure to divide them.

Relief flooded his eyes. "No. Tell me all about her."

Frankly, she was disappointed in herself for not having thought of this story sooner. The fact that his mentor had stolen and plundered her great-grandmother's broach was sure to push them back on the opposite shores where they belonged.

So, while enjoying the delicate fish, rice and fruit on her plate, Brenna shared the story of her grandmother's fateful Atlantic crossing.

Surprisingly, the mention of Dan Loff, his friend and mentor, didn't bring a spark of pride to Gavin's eyes. Instead, his jaw tightened.

"I'm sorry for your family's loss," he said. "The broach should have been turned over to you."

"Were you part of that search?"

"No."

The knots in her stomach loosened slightly. She wasn't sure why it mattered. Loff had still been his mentor. Gavin's tendency to sell off the artifacts still annoyed her. But if she had the hots, even reluctantly, for a man who'd actually been part of her family tragedy, she was sure she'd be physically ill.

"Have you ever broken apart jewelry you found in a dig or dive?"

"No," he said, sounding oddly reluctant.

"But you've been with Loff when he did."

"Yes."

"Do you agree with the practice?"

"No."

"I assumed you did."

"I figured." He refilled their wineglasses, then took a sip as if he, too, needed a minute to gather himself. Was there any chance he was thinking about the families through history who'd endured a loss and never had a funeral to attend or a grave to visit? Was he considering how difficult it was to imagine your loved one's last, terrified, hopeless moments?

Did he feel the loss of the great heroes of the past as profoundly as she did?

Taking his wine with him, he slid from the booth and wandered across the cabin. He pushed open the glass door and stood in the opening, staring up at the sky. "I love the sea," he said quietly. "I grew up in Austin, but my family always went to the beach for vacations." He sighed. "I was hooked. My first love."

So she'd been right about the Texas accent. But he'd taken elaborate steps to hide his past. Why was he sharing it now?

"Water and sand?" She rose from the table and followed him. "I figured you for the D-cup variety of passion."

"That came later." He shook his head. "A lot later. I was pretty shy as a teen, so I was devoted to comic books, science and history. I enjoyed learning, and I thought if I was smart enough, Debbie Pendleton would talk to me."

"Did she?"

"No. I told her I enjoyed learning."

"Intelligence is a blessing," Brenna said.

He looked at her. "Is that what you tell the unpopular geeks at Palmer's Island High?"

"*Geek* is derogatory. These are the future rulers of our country."

He remained silent, apparently not believing her any more than the kids did.

"Yes, that's what I tell them—when they'll listen to me, which is rarely." She joined him in the doorway, leaning back against the metal frame. The sky was clear and lovely, the stars infinite. And he'd never been more appealing. "My general mantra is 'don't peak at seventeen.'"

"That's a good one. My parents preferred 'do well in college, or we'll make you renovate the basement.'" He smiled as he said the words.

"What do they do?"

"Work hard. At least nine months of the year, then they float around all summer. They cruise the Gulf, head down to Mexico, turn around and come back."

Brenna suddenly understood this was his version of an apology. His lucrative work had allowed him to support his parents' dreams. And while that didn't excuse some of the things he'd done, she recognized that much.

He might be an arrogant skirt-chaser on the surface, but there was something of value underneath.

"Sounds lovely," she said. "My parents are on a month-long cruise right now, but they're generally content here."

"Here's pretty nice."

"Yeah. Summer is brutally hot, though."

"Tell me about it. Miami is the same."

"I generally try to go to—" She stopped. "Are we actually talking about the weather?"

"It's a nice, safe subject."

"And you're a nice, safe guy?"

"Yes. No," he immediately corrected.

She smiled. "There's that split personality I'm so wild about."

His gaze locked with hers. He set his glass on the counter by the sink, then moved toward her. "So I'm hot and crazy."

"I couldn't have said it better myself."

He traced the tip of his finger along her jaw. "And you have the hots for me. Does that make you nuts, too?"

Her heartbeat quickened. "Definitely."

His gaze dropped to her lips. "It's nice not to be alone. Especially with someone as unbalanced as I am."

"I'm not sure—"

He silenced her with a kiss, and she didn't hesitate to lean into him, sliding her hands up his chest.

All thoughts of mistakes and questionable sanity fled with his fervent touch. He grasped her tight against his body. Heat pumped off him, infusing her with his excitement and need. She could feel the hard edge of his erection pressing against her belly, and her body answered with a rush of desire.

As he trailed his mouth down her throat, she angled her head for easier access and gripped his arms. The feel of the hard muscle beneath her hands sent a new wave of excitement cascading over her.

She recalled the day they'd met, when he'd walked through this very cabin fresh from his shower and shirtless. She'd wanted his body nearly as much as she wanted to understand the complex man who inhabited it.

He panted against her skin. "If you're planning to tell me I'm a lecherous pig, you'd better do it fast."

"Actually, I'm pretty speechless."

His lips parted in a quick grin, then he was kissing her again. The taste of him was glorious. The woodsy, citrus scent surrounded her, enticing her to get closer.

Because of the difference in their heights, he had to bend practically in half to reach her. As she was about to suggest they solve their dilemma by sitting—or lying—down, he wrapped his arms around her waist and picked her up, carrying her toward the back of the cabin and into the bedroom.

A large bed with a navy spread dominated the room, and the only light came from a small window through which the moon cast its haunting glow.

She had little interest in the ambience, since Gavin was backing toward the bed and pulling her with him. When he sat, she stood between his legs. The position put them on an even level.

The gold in his eyes gleamed with hunger and possession. Brenna sensed an enticing kind of danger, like an antelope faced with a lion.

Belying the intensity in his expression, he cupped his hands on either side of her face and kissed her gently, as if he wanted to savor each movement, each touch and sensation.

Pleasure skated from her head to her toes, along with an unfamiliar wave of tenderness. Her heart thrummed in panic. This was a chemical thing between them. They weren't in a relationship.

Before she could fully think through her concerns, he untied her halter top, exposing her to the waist. His eyes popped wide when he realized she wasn't wearing a bra underneath.

"You're beautiful," he said, his tone nearly reverent as he glided the back of his hand over her breast and down her stomach.

The muscles low in her abdomen clenched, then pulsed.

She should be self-conscious. He was practically a stranger. But she wasn't uncomfortable. She was fascinated.

By him. By the sensations he inspired.

Grabbing the hem of his T-shirt, she pulled it up and over his head. She trailed her fingertips lightly across his cheek and into his hair, where she pulled out the band binding it. The sun-kissed locks fell nearly to his shoulders.

Again, the comparison to the pirates that had scourged and ruled the seas hundreds of years before passed through her mind. She could easily envision him standing defiantly on the bow of a grand ship as it cut through the wild ocean waves toward exotic adventure.

Unable to resist, she traced her hand across his deeply tanned, muscled chest. His skin was harder than hers, but smooth and warm.

He was beautiful.

Before she could tell him so, he jerked her into his lap. Their bare chests met, and her nipples puckered.

The rest of their clothes wound up on the floor very quickly.

Naked, she climbed on top of him, straddling his hips as she rolled on the condom he provided. He braced his hands at her waist and lifted her slightly, then she seated herself on his erection, gasping as her body clenched around him.

Leaning forward, she pressed her lips to his, the taste and feel of him sending pulses of need and anticipation flying all over her body. Their hips rocked together in a primal and natural dance as old as time. He clutched her against him as their hearts raced and chased pleasure.

The buzz of desire filled her ears. He seemed to fill and surround her at the same time. She'd never felt such intensity. She couldn't stop touching him. Didn't want him to stop touching her.

Her lips trailed across his heated flesh. His teeth scraped her throat. And as every part of him bonded with every part of her, she couldn't escape the words of Yeats—the poem of the mermaid, how even as happiness descends on lovers they can surely drown.

So she finally understood the overwhelming sensation of hunger and compulsion for fulfillment. For the need to give and be consumed completely.

Sex had always been nice and straightforward. This was something else entirely. This was what drove poets to pen and singers to strive for a high F.

The crash happened suddenly. One second she was holding her breath, the next she couldn't catch it. Pulses of satisfaction rippled everywhere. He clutched her hips as, he, too, reached the peak. She gripped a fistful of his hair, buried her face against his neck and relished the gratification they'd created.

She collapsed on top of his sweat-slicked chest, his heartbeat sprinting against her ear.

Her conscience was sure to awaken soon. But at the moment, cocooned in the darkness of his bedroom, enjoying the warmth and intimacy of his body, she could find no regret.

PENELOPE WATERS WAS having carnal thoughts about a man.

She closed her eyes as she tried to remember the Wordsworth

poem she and Miss McGary had discussed earlier, the last HTML script she'd created, a Psalm, Sister Mary Katherine's disapproving face…anything.

"Are you all right?"

Peeking through her lids, she studied Finn Hastings—the spiky, sun-kissed hair, piercing pale blue eyes and lean body. Okay. Major carnal thoughts. "I'm fine," she managed to say.

With a shrug, Finn licked his chocolate ice cream cone.

Relieved the attention was off her for the moment, Penelope spooned up another bite of her peach-flavored scoop.

After she and Finn had left Dr. Fortune's boat, he'd offered to take her on a few more of his local "check-ins" before taking her back to her apartment in Charleston, only a bridge and a few miles away from the island. Dazzled by the rebel-looking, yet khaki-uniform-clad Finn, Penelope had smiled and nodded.

How she could comfortably talk to Dr. Fortune about complex underwater robots and the computers that controlled them, but not be able to so much as bat her lashes at a hot guy her age, seemed to be the sad story of Penelope's social life.

Shy, smart girls who wore glasses and understood computers really well weren't exactly part of the popular teen parade.

Thankfully, check-ins turned out to be Finn visiting local businesses to make sure they were happy with beach security and the general welfare of the town. Since Penelope knew many business owners—and had installed most of their computer systems—she felt reasonably comfortable.

Now, though, she and Finn were alone at the ice cream shop next to the pier, and she had zero to say.

"Did you spend too much time on the beach today?" he asked.

She generally turned into a tomato when she spent more than twenty minutes in the sun. As a result of that genetic defect, plus the skin-cancer folks advocating protection for everybody, she was a staunch advocate of fifty-plus sunscreen. "No. Why?"

"Your face is red."

Oh, gee, how great. In fact, could this date/encounter/ moment-after-check-ins get any better?

"You have really great eyes. Do you always hide behind those big glasses?"

Oh, gee, apparently it could.

But at the same instant embarrassment rolled over her, she remembered the Sisters constant litany about respecting herself—head to toe, body and mind. "I need glasses to see," she said, pushing aside her dessert and clenching a napkin in her hand. "They're not a fashion accessory, a vanity or a shield."

"They have contacts now."

"I have them. I just happen to not be wearing them at the moment."

He grinned as he bit into his cone. "You're also really hot."

Speechless, Penelope stared at him. "With or without the glasses?"

"Either way."

"So why did you bring it up?"

"I like to see you blushing and indignant."

"When have you ever seen me blushing and indignant?"

"Twenty seconds ago."

"Before that."

"Well, there was that town hall meeting a few months ago, about the city providing free Wi-Fi access for restaurants and shops near the pier to boost business. Your presentation was organized and persuasive."

Penelope blinked. A guy who thought she was hot and respected her intelligence? Where had he come from? "Oh. Thanks."

"What are you studying in school?"

"Computer science." Inevitably, this announcement caused

hot guys to search the area around her for an equally hot girl, or express a sudden interest in getting tech support.

Finn Hastings simply nodded. "Smart. You obviously have a talent for computers. Plus, the job market's bound to be good."

"I had an offer from a tech company in San Francisco to do a summer internship."

He looked surprised. "Why didn't you go?"

"The historical society needed me." She felt heat again rise up her neck. "And I missed the island."

"You live in an apartment twelve miles from here."

"But I barely get over here twice a month. I'm always in class or working."

"Where do you work?"

"For myself," she said, lifting her chin with pride. "I have a web design business."

"The sheriff's site could use some work. I'll mention it to him. Maybe I can get you some more business."

Penelope blinked. "Thanks."

Had he always been this nice? Since she and Finn were personal projects of Sister Mary Katherine, they'd spent a little time together over the last few years. But he'd never so much as let their eyes meet for more than a second before today, whereas she'd always found him dangerously attractive. Was that because he was an ex-con, or because he was just... him?

"You know you can do your work anywhere," he continued. "Bring your laptop over and sit at Gilda's bakery, using the Wi-Fi you got the city to pay for."

"I guess I could. Are you always so direct?"

"Yes."

"Good to know. Why did you steal that car?"

His lips turned up on one side. "Which one?"

A bubble of nervousness blossomed in her stomach. "There was more than one?"

"Oh, yeah." His gaze moved to hers and held. "You sure you want to hear this?"

No. She swallowed hard. "Yes."

"It won't take long. It's not even very interesting." He tossed his napkin in a nearby trash can. "I didn't want to study or follow my parents' rules, so I joined a gang. They were my family, and to prove my loyalty I had to steal." He lifted his shoulders in a jerky shrug. "I was good at cars."

"But you got arrested."

"I wasn't that good."

"And now you're a deputy."

"My sister threatened to kick my ass if I screwed up again."

"Plus, it's handy that she's married to the sheriff."

Finn's gaze bored into Penelope's. "Are you asking me if I'm using my position in the sheriff's office to continue my criminal past?"

"No." Impulsively, she placed her hand on his forearm. "It's just…you know, a big turnaround, and I—"

He linked their hands by threading his fingers through hers. "Prison isn't pretty. I'm not doing anything that would send me back. Ever."

She could feel his pulse hammering against hers. And though their discussion was certainly serious, all she could think about was the fact that he was touching her.

Finally.

When he continued, his voice had dropped an octave. "And my parents died in a car wreck while I was in prison. They never saw me being somebody. The least I can do is to erase the mistakes that made them ashamed."

"I don't even remember my last conversation with my parents. I barely remember them at all."

"But you still want them to be proud."

"More than anything. So I believe you. That you changed your life, I mean," she all but whispered.

"Why?"

"Because you like to see me blushing and indignant."

A full smile rose on his face. "Yes, I do."

"Do you really think I'd look better without glasses?"

He closed one eye, studying her. Then, with his free hand, he pulled off her glasses. As he set them on the table, his thumb brushed her cheek, and though the evening temperature still hovered in the mid-eighties, she shivered.

"I like that I can see the stars in your eyes," he said.

"Stars? Is that some kind of line?"

"I don't do lines. It's true. You have cognac-colored stars in the center of your eyes. They're pretty amazing."

"Cognac?"

"Brandy. It's a reddish-goldish brown."

"I know what it is. I just never pictured you as a brandy drinker."

"I'm not. Tried it once. Tastes like cough syrup. But the sheriff has a bottle in the conference room that the mayor gave him for Christmas last year. Mostly we use it to calm down hysterical people. Usually the mayor himself."

"Does that happen often?"

He nodded. "His golf game was really shaky this past spring."

"Isn't it always?"

"Probably."

How they'd gone from her appeal with or without the ability to see, to the mayor's obsession with golf, she wasn't sure. But her nerves had probably gotten in the way somehow.

The story of her life.

"So no glasses?" she asked after polishing off her ice cream.

He returned the frames to her face. "I think you're amazing either way."

Did he? This whole thing had come out of left field. She'd never imagined he thought anything at all about her. The conversation was surreal; yet there was something lovely and wonderful and scary at the same time. "I think I'm pretty ordinary."

"You're not looking hard enough."

Even as her heart skipped a beat, she forced herself to look directly at him. "And you are? Looking, I mean."

"Yes."

"So why haven't you ever told me this before? You seem to go out of your way to ignore me most of the time."

"Sister Mary Katherine glares at me when I look at you."

Embarrassment yet again washed over Penelope. "She's very protective."

"She should be. You trust too easily." Still holding her hand, he stood. His thumb skimmed across her knuckles. "You want to go for a walk on the beach?"

Definitely.

But she also wanted to understand what was happening to her.

His interest seemed a gift she wasn't sure she was ready to accept. Plus, as much as she'd been schooled in the ways of divine intervention, and the symbiotic relationship of them both losing their parents at a critical stage, she hesitated to take the next step. She wanted her independence, but she'd been insulated all her life. Though they were only two years apart in age, could she really handle a guy—a *man*—like Finn?

Unsure of the answer, she cast a glance at the horizon.

The sun had started its descent, casting a pink-and-purple haze on the sky. How many times had she been at a beach party and fantasized about a guy sitting with her, just at the shore, his arms wrapped around her from behind as he told her half the things Finn had just shared?

How many times had she longed to be part of a couple? How many times had she longed not to be alone?

Squeezing his hand, she rose. "I'd love to walk on the beach with you."

5

GAVIN SLID HIS HAND DOWN Brenna's silky, bare backside with a sigh of satisfaction.

It had been way too long since that kind of intense pleasure had crossed his path.

Despite his reputation, he spent most nights alone. Casual sex with women who cared for little except his money and celebrity had lost its allure some time ago. And because of his reputation, the rest of the women weren't interested in him.

What the smart, feisty and beautiful Brenna saw in him, he hadn't a clue.

Holding on to her would be another thing entirely.

As he wrapped his arm around her waist and tucked her beneath his shoulder, positioning them so they lay alongside each other, doubts invaded his blissful thoughts.

She was strong and true, and he was living a lie. She taught high school literature on a quiet South Carolina island; he had a modern condo in Miami he hardly saw, and courted the media as practically a full-time occupation. In academic circles, she was respected. He was a novelty.

Not only didn't they mix, they didn't live in the same universe.

"I should probably go," she said, her breath brushing his shoulder.

Despite all the logical reasons to do the contrary, he contracted his arm around her waist. "You don't have to."

She trailed her fingertips over his chest, then abruptly withdrew her hand. "I'd like to sit up."

He let go of her, and she pushed up, tucking the sheet around her. With her bright hair tousled around her beautifully pale face, he had to fist his hands to keep from burying his fingers in the waving flames.

"I need to go," she said.

Why? he wanted to ask. Though he knew.

Instead, he searched his normally quick brain for a logical reason to hold her. He chose the primary thing that stood between them, which he'd probably regret, but what else did he have?

"Can I show you what I found today?" he asked her.

"Found where?"

"At the wreck site." He swung his legs to the floor. "You're one of the few people who'll truly appreciate it."

Though she seemed wary, he managed to get on a pair of jeans, convinced her to wear her clothes plus one of his old Cambridge sweatshirts—which, thankfully, she didn't scoff at. He led her out to the deck, where he had several brass buttons soaking in a chemical solution that would remove a hundred-plus years of salt water residue and restore the relics to their former glory.

"What are they?" she asked, leaning over the solution tray.

"Buttons. Off a uniform coat, probably. We're not sure whether it was Union, Confederate or just random. The pattern should be clear by tomorrow."

"You can make it shiny again?"

"Yeah." He glanced at her pale face, noted the shock and horror in her eyes and realized regret was only seconds away. "Pretty cool, don't you think?"

"They belonged to someone," she murmured.

"Sure they did, but—"

"The buttons *belonged* to someone," she repeated, her fierce gaze locking with his. "Someone's father, someone's husband, someone's brother or sister. How can you just pick it up like a shell you found on the shore?"

"I dove three hundred feet to find it. And nobody would ever see it if I hadn't done so."

"Exactly. The sea claimed the button, as it claimed the coat, as it claimed the owner. We have no right to disturb that cycle."

He'd had enough of her self-righteous anger—even though he now understood the source of it. "How will we ever learn from the past if we don't explore it?"

"Lincoln referred to the dead of the Civil War as giving *the last full measure of devotion.* You really want to stir their graves so you can show the world their buttons?"

"You're quoting Lincoln? He was on the other side."

"The other side of what?"

"The Civil War."

Again, Gavin had taken a serious misstep. She poked her finger in his chest so hard he backed up. "He was our *president.* And a great humanitarian."

"I know. I just—"

"He also said, 'A house divided against itself cannot stand.' He understood, as few during that time seemed to, that the country had to mend itself. We had to be one nation again—at all costs."

And what a cost it had been.

Yet another reason Gavin needed to be around people like Brenna. People who knew and respected history, and their ancestors, while still understanding the mistakes that had been made.

He was also smart enough to recognize that she wasn't only talking about the division of war in general, but the one between them, as well. They were on different sides of a critical issue, one he didn't see them ever breaching.

"Lincoln was a wise man," he said, figuring that was one of the few statements she couldn't argue with.

She turned away. "I have to go."

He grabbed her hand and held her in place. "I wish you wouldn't."

"We— I made a mistake. I don't do this."

"Do what?"

"Sleep with men I don't know."

"You're one of the few people who may actually know me."

Full of confusion and doubt, her gaze met his before jumping away. "But I don't."

He let go of her hand. "You want me to follow you home?"

"No. I just live a few blocks away."

He acknowledged he had no idea where. He didn't even have her number.

"I guess I'll—" She stopped and cleared her throat. "Bye."

He watched her leave, and though he wanted to go after her more than anything, he remained rooted to the spot.

She was wise to leave. After all, what kind of man was he to hold on to?

"I'm thinking about retiring," Gavin said two days later, as he leaned back in his deck lounge chair.

At the other end of the cell phone connection, his agent and close friend, Jeff Hannah, sighed. "We've been through this three times this month already."

"I'm serious this time."

"It must really suck to be you—rich, successful, popular, smart, chick-magnet. Man, how do you have the strength to crawl out of bed every morning?"

"I want to write a book."

"So start typing."

Watching the sky turn pink, Gavin kept calm but infused

his tone with steel. *"The Carolina*'s going to be my last project for a while, Jeff."

"Sorry, buddy. The other side of the Atlantic calls. You're already contracted to find the *Star of Ariana* for Lord Westmore."

"Pablo can do it."

"They want you."

Why? Gavin wondered. Though, unfortunately, he knew.

"Finding the infamous ruby for Westmore will be the perfect storyline for the reality show one of the TV networks is offering," Jeff continued.

"No," Gavin said. "No way."

"Didn't figure you'd go for it," Jeff muttered. "Which is why I instead agreed to an interview by *World Adventure* magazine. The reporter will be by at two on Thursday."

"Whatever."

"Your team is saving history—you make a difference. Do you really want to leave these projects vulnerable to the treasure vultures?"

Guilt tightened Gavin's gut. "No. But I can't go on forever like this, pretending to be Gavin Fortune."

"Hell. Forever? You're only thirty-four."

"Sometimes I feel a hundred."

"Because you spend too much time holed up in that cabin. Why don't you get out and actually have some of the fun you're notorious for?"

"I have a presentation at a local college."

"So impress a few of the nubile students, ask one of them out for a drink. Impress her with your mind and dimples while you enjoy her agile body."

Thinking of agile bodies only made Gavin think of Brenna. Why would he want to fool around with a college kid when he could have her?

You don't have her.

"What a great idea," he said with no enthusiasm.

"If I wasn't doing actual work, I'd come be your wingman."

"I do actual work."

"Sure, you do. Swimming, diving and playing with underwater robots. I knew I should have paid more attention in science class instead of focusing on contract law."

Despite his frustration, Gavin found the energy to smile. "You're in the right business. Besides, somebody has to protect my amoral empire."

"Naturally. In fact, I should give myself a raise."

"Yeah. You go do that."

Gavin disconnected, feeling better than he had when he'd called, but still unsettled.

Would he disappoint himself—and Brenna—even more by retiring? Could he leave the world's treasures unprotected from the corrupt hands of Dan Loff and others like him?

Was one woman really that important?

"THANKS, MABEL," Brenna said as she handed her empty plate to the diner owner. "You were right about the marinated pork chop."

"Aren't I always?"

Mabel's Diner was an institution, and Mabel and her staff of Southern cooks brought a whole new meaning to comforting soul food. Her cola cake was rumored to have cured two people of cancer, and was guaranteed to throw even the most stringent of dieters off their low cal, low sugar commitments with a mere whiff of its chocolatey goodness.

She wondered if she could lure Gavin Fortune and his crew into ceasing their hunt with a bribe of cake.

Gee, girl, that's probably a record. She glanced at her watch for confirmation. *Wow. You've gone a whole four minutes without thinking about him.*

"You havin' any trouble with those treasure people?"

Brenna turned on her stool and looked up, way up, into

the face of Sloan's father, Buddy Caldwell, local legend and retired island sheriff. "No, sir."

As Buddy pulled off his ever-present Stetson and slid onto the stool next to Brenna, he gave Mabel a crooked smile. It was an open secret that they were dating, though they always claimed to be long-time widowers who'd simply become friends.

While Sloan thought the ruse was silly, Brenna found their decorum charming. Gavin could put down his latest press release and learn a thing or two in that regard.

Twenty seconds that time. How embarrassing. It was as if she couldn't forget him. As if she hadn't had a one-night stand in a while.

You haven't, her libido reminded her. *In fact, you can add up your grand, lifetime total to one.*

"I saw Deputy Hastings yesterday," Buddy said, thankfully breaking into her self-absorbance. "He said he'd stopped by their boat."

"Yeah. I appreciate the sheriff's office checking in." And from Penelope's blushing smile yesterday, she was appreciative, as well. "I wish they could arrest somebody for something, though."

Buddy accepted the mug of coffee Mabel set in front of him. "Sloan said you don't agree with their explorin'."

"Grave robbing," Brenna muttered.

In his calm, controlled way, Buddy nodded. "Then again, an exhibition of their finds could be an honor for the island."

"But there won't be an exhibition. They'll sell off the artifacts like used car parts at the junkyard."

"I hear they have that reputation." He sipped his coffee. "If only somebody could change their mind, remind them how important their exploration is to our island."

"That's what I'm trying to do."

"Yeah?" The pale blue eyes his daughter had inherited flashed with fake surprise. "Well, then, everything should be fine."

"It's not," Brenna said, barely avoiding snapping. "They're not really listening."

"They? Or him?"

"Both. And he leads them."

"I hear he's qualified."

"He's certainly experienced." She had Penelope continuing to search for Gavin Anybody and his doctorates. That fake last name thing was a real problem, though.

"An intelligent man respects the opinion of others."

"He respects. He just doesn't agree."

"Convince him."

As if it was so simple. Frankly, she was tired of worrying about, thinking about and obsessing about Gavin Fortune. She reached into her purse to pay her tab. "Any time you want to give me a hand, Sheriff, jump right in."

"I am."

His quiet, though considerable, support was appreciated. But she and Gavin were past conversational solutions. Avoidance was probably best.

And yet she didn't want that, either.

The bliss they'd shared, the connection between them—neither was normal. Or easily dismissed. *Irresistible* came to mind.

But how could she trade her conscience for passion?

Her friend's father certainly didn't deserve the brunt of her frustration. "I appreciate your support, sir. I'll keep—"

"Dr. Loff, what are your plans for Palmer's Island?"

Whirling, Brenna unbelievably saw Dr. Dan Loff walking through the diner's front door.

A reporter walked backward in front of him, a microphone extended. To the side, a cameraman recorded every move.

While every eye in the restaurant turned to him, Loff moved to a booth and sat down, never once glancing around. He picked up a menu and studied it.

What the hell was going on?

One of Mabel's waitresses cautiously approached Loff's table. He smiled blindingly, and Brenna flinched.

The smile was familiar. It was the one she'd seen in many pictures of Gavin. Not the same face surrounded it, of course. But the sentiment was the same.

Indulgent. Charming. Fake.

"An interesting performance," Buddy Caldwell said quietly. "Do you need me to jump in again?"

"I'm not sure," Brenna said slowly, her gaze still glued to Loff's table.

What was he doing here? Had Gavin called him?

Her heart lurched at the thought.

Despite their supposedly close relationship, Gavin didn't have much to say about his mentor. He had, in fact, apologized for him.

From somewhere, logic filtered in.

Loff must have hired the film crew to pose as media. Or paid a reporter to follow him. Sunken ships carrying hundred-plus-year-old treasure were minor news, a cute toss-in to serious stories about politics, the economy and crime. Maybe a feature on the Discovery Channel would surface. But the idea that a legitimate news crew would follow Loff into Mabel's Diner willingly—even if he'd announced he was about to hold up the place at gunpoint—was laughable.

"Maybe they found the treasure chest," Buddy said.

"That doesn't explain why Loff is here. He's not part of this project." And she had a really bad feeling about his presence. "I need to go." She laid money on the counter for Mabel, thanked Buddy for his support and scooted out the door.

All the way to the marina, she kept telling herself to calm down. Loff had probably just come to help Gavin. Maybe he'd shown up simply to mooch off *The Carolina*'s publicity.

No big deal.

Still, she quickened her step as she approached Gavin's boat. The only person she saw on board was Pablo. "Where's Gavin?" she asked him, careful to keep her tone calm.

"Giving a lecture at the College of Charleston."

Her stomach bottomed out. "He's not here?"

Pablo glanced at his watch. "He's due back in about an hour or so." He smiled with considerable charm. "I'd be glad to entertain you until he gets back."

"I've got to talk to him right away."

"Something wrong?"

"Dan Loff is on Palmer's Island."

Pablo's expression turned to stone.

Relief washed over Brenna. "You didn't know."

"How would I?"

"Gavin didn't call him?"

"No!"

Something odd was definitely going on between Gavin and Loff. "I thought Loff was his mentor. Aren't they good friends?"

"You should really have this conversation with the boss."

Brenna crossed her arms over her chest. "Why? What's going on?"

"Let me get you a lounge chair and a beer. You can relax till Gavin arrives."

"No, thanks. I'll go to him. The College of Charleston?"

"Yeah. Historic preservation building."

"Thanks."

She'd turned to leave when she heard his voice from behind her. "You shouldn't give the boss a hard time, *cariña*. Those boys are long since dust."

She looked at him over her shoulder. "Exactly. That's why I have to protect them. Those boys don't have anybody else."

He simply nodded.

Back in her car, Brenna left the island, driving over the bridge to Charleston, then on, into the downtown core of the city.

Since it was Monday evening, she had little trouble finding a parking space reasonably close to the historic preservation building on Bull Street.

She wondered how she'd find the right classroom, but as soon as she walked through the door, she nearly ran into a huge brass easel holding a poster of the gorgeous and smiling face of Dr. Gavin Fortune.

Naturally.

The man's ego really was a bit too healthy.

She followed the sign's directions to a large lecture hall whose double doors were wide open. In the darkened room, Brenna was able to slip into the back row.

Standing behind a podium on a brightly lit stage, his hair tied back at the nape of his neck, Gavin was talking about the War of 1812 and its effects on America and Europe. Though she briefly wondered what in the world he was doing giving a speech instead of romancing the bikini-clad population of Palmer's Island, she found herself getting lost in his subject.

As expected, he spoke with confidence and was easy on the eyes, but her interest went beyond the man himself. His words and tone were reverent and engaging. The passionate sparks in his eyes were captivating. It was obvious he was extremely intelligent and thoughtful. Maybe the degrees *were* real.

And yet he didn't talk like a scholar with lofty words and a self-important tone.

It was sort of like watching a gifted actor who understood not just how to perform, but his subject matter, too. Someone who believed absolutely in what he was saying all the more because he'd lived it.

This was the man she'd sensed behind the playboy image.

And she fell just a little in love with him at every word.

Oh, no, she didn't. To stifle a gasp, she literally clapped her hand over her mouth, causing a group of girls in the row in front of her to turn and glare.

What Brenna felt was simple attraction. A crush. Chemistry. Intense chemistry, perhaps. But still a physical thing. Only now it was coupled with a mental thing. And, together, those things were a huge thing.

She pressed her lips together. *O-kay.* That train of thought was really embarrassing. Thankfully, only herself, her libido and her conscience had heard the slip.

"So, now that I'm done with my academic droning," Gavin said, walking from behind the podium to rest against its side. "Questions?"

Of course there were questions. Mostly from nervous female students who wanted to hear tales of the adventure and romance of treasure hunting.

While Brenna had spent most of her time arguing with him about treasure and the merits of hunting it, she could vouch for the romance. Even the regret over their night together was fading. Maybe one-night stands weren't her usual format, but watching Gavin's dimpled smile flash, she was beginning to come to terms with the inspiration that had caused her to swing a hard left.

Gavin was politely teasing and sometimes mysterious about answering the questions, including the one that asked if he was personally unattached. He bore no resemblance to the amoral playboy his reputation dictated. The forward and obvious come-ons he'd used on Brenna when they'd first met were absent.

Because he didn't feel right about using them on college students? Or because they weren't really part of him?

When the discussion ended, several students approached the stage, forming a line to ask questions and, in many cases, request that Gavin sign copies of his latest book.

Brenna walked down the stairs toward the group, but hung back from joining them. Regardless of her mixed feelings about him, she wasn't about to pick an argument in so public a forum. Whatever their differences, she had no right to embarrass him.

Then, without warning, his gaze found hers.

Shock, then pleasure flitted across his face. And still he stared.

The students in front of him actually turned to see what he found so fascinating.

Brenna kept her attention on Gavin and prayed her face wasn't turning red.

He finally broke their connection, and she inched her way closer as he concluded his discussion with the students. It wasn't until she was a few feet away that she remembered why she'd come.

Dan Loff. Her nemesis. His mentor.

Broaching this subject was going to be dicey at best.

By the time she reached him, he was sitting on the edge of the stage and talking to an attractive blonde.

"We meet at the Sky Bar on Thursday nights," she was saying.

Gavin raised his eyebrows in that charming expression he used as easily as he breathed. In his jeans, T-shirt and wrinkly sport coat, he could have been any random college professor. Well, if the teacher was as hot as the sun and twice as magnetic. "History majors who meet at a bar?"

"Serious discussions and fruity drinks," the student said encouragingly. "Smart and fun."

"I was definitely born in the wrong decade," Gavin murmured. "Thanks for the invite. The recovery of *The Carolina* takes up most of my time, but I'll try to stop by."

"Great. See ya."

The blonde turned, her curious gaze sweeping Brenna, then she moved past her and up the stairs.

"Learn anything?" Gavin asked as soon as the student was out of earshot.

"Definitely." About herself, him and history all at the same time.

"Wanna go get a drink and talk about it?"

"Sure. Know any good bars around here?"

Grinning, Gavin hitched a worn, brown leather briefcase on his shoulder. "I think Joe's might suit us better."

Brenna thought of Loff sitting in a booth at Mabel's. So

close. How long before somebody told him about Coconut Joe's? "I was thinking of somewhere a little more private."

"Oh, yeah?" Golden sparks lit Gavin's hazel eyes. He extended his arm toward the doorway. "Lead on, my Irish pixie. Lead on."

SHE TOOK HIM TO HER HOUSE, where her cat decided he was Andrew Jackson and Gavin was the British Empire.

"I don't like the way he stares at me," Gavin said, sitting at one end of Brenna's sofa, while the cat in question perched threateningly on the coffee table in front of him.

"Cats stare," Brenna said as she handed him a glass of red wine. "It's their way of showing dominance."

Gavin suppressed a shiver as he looked into the golden eyes of Shakespeare Fuzzyboots. Who, despite his silly name and soft-looking orange-and-white fur, clearly had evil intentions toward other males invading his domain. "It's working."

"Be nice, Shakes," Brenna said.

The cat, who couldn't possibly understand English—well, maybe—cocked his head at his mistress, gave her a baleful stare, then obediently hopped onto the chair adjacent to the sofa.

Gavin had no doubt the feline was still planning to keep a close eye on him.

Wise move, since Gavin was planning to seduce his mistress at the first opportunity. Did cats sense pheromones?

"We need to talk," Brenna said as she smoothed her hands down her bright yellow sundress and sat beside him on the couch.

"That'll be a nice change. You've been ignoring me for two days."

"I had my reasons."

Yeah. He was well aware of their differences. Just as he had no idea how to get past them. Stalling, he sipped his wine, which was complex, fruity and spicy.

Much like the woman who'd served it to him.

"Could we steer away from the subject of *The Carolina?*" he asked. "That tends to get us into trouble."

"Then our talk is going to be really brief."

He had other plans for her lips, anyway. "Fine by me."

"How've you been? The weather's nice."

"It's July in South Carolina. It's hot as hell."

Drinking from her wineglass, she shrugged. "You could be in Minnesota."

"It's beautiful in Minnesota this time of year."

"No kidding? Why were you lecturing at the college? I assumed you spent your free time in nude beach volleyball tournaments."

"I do, but the island ordinances are tricky to get around. We have to wait till nightfall."

She glanced at her watch. "You'd better get going then or you'll be late."

"You invited me to your place and offered me a drink. It would be rude to leave so soon."

"How about we sit here silently and see who among the three of us can stare the others down? First one to blink loses."

"The three of us?"

"We'll get Shakes in on the game."

Gavin glanced over at the cat, who was sitting still as a statue, his tail curled around his fluffy body as he regarded them with his defiant and superior expression.

"My money's on him, by the way," Brenna added.

"This is a very strange conversation."

"No, this is a very boring conversation." She sipped her wine. "Your choice."

No talking about *The Carolina*. Fine. He could talk about the War of 1812. No, he'd done that already. Once a day was probably enough.

Come to think of it, why had she been at his lecture? Only Pablo could have told her where he was.

"What did Pablo tell you?" Gavin asked, bracing himself.

His first mate seemed determined to be both matchmaker and competitor when it came to Brenna.

"I thought you didn't want to talk about—"

"What did he tell you about my presentation at the college?"

"That you had one and where it was being held."

"Nothing else?"

Brenna's gaze slid to his. "He also advised me to go easy on you."

"Is that why you invited me to your place?"

"No."

The house was small, but had a lot of color and personality. Again, much like its owner.

Pictures and books dominated the built-in bookcases. The couch where they sat was lime-green with red and purple pillows. The chair the cat perched on was purple. The dark oak floor was shiny and spotless.

And he was stalling again.

Hadn't he always faced consequences and challenges—no matter how difficult? Hadn't he proved, especially to himself, that he could make the tough decisions?

He set his wine on the coffee table. "Why did Pablo want you to go easy on me? And *The Carolina* is no longer off-limits."

"He wanted me to realize that history is just that—past and gone."

"You know that already."

"Yeah, but I do dwell a lot."

He laid his arm along the back of the sofa and scooted closer to her. That admission alone was a big concession. And if he wanted the peace to continue, he knew he needed to contradict much of what she thought she knew about him.

She'd trusted him with her past, why she felt so compelled to fight against him. It was time he gave her at least that much in return. "I went to the college tonight because I like lecturing."

"And learning."

He grasped her hand, sliding his thumb back and forth across her knuckles. "That, too."

"And chasing hot girls in bikinis on the beach."

"Mmm...not so much."

"Your image is fake."

Pleased she'd grasped the point so quickly, he nodded. "Pretty much."

"Why did you change your name?"

"Because I had to protect my parents and hide my academic record to fully become Gavin Fortune." He met her gaze directly. "My last name is Randall. My family is wealthy and well-known, so—"

"Hang on," Brenna interrupted. "You don't finance their sailing trips?"

"No. There's plenty of disposable funds in the Randall family coffers for sailing."

She clenched her hand around his. "Oh, man. I just got it. Austin, big-time wealth. You're talking about the Randall family as in the Randall Foundation Cancer Research Center."

"Yes."

Her eyes widened. "And the Randall Literacy Center."

He nodded. "Ten locations nationwide. My great-grandfather started that. Everybody else since then has only expanded it."

"You're rich. I mean megarich."

Something about her resigned tone made him smile. "Gavin Fortune hasn't done too bad for himself. My family is something else entirely."

"You're not going to start talking about yourself in the third person now, are you?"

"No."

"And your degrees are real."

"Yes."

So he told her.

Excellence and generosity were expected in his family.

When he was young, he'd excelled at school. After skipping grades and entering college early, he'd buried himself in science and history. For the first time in his life, he'd been both challenged and fascinated, instead of intimidated by the idea of following in his family's illustrious footsteps. His love for the ocean eventually took precedence, and as he finished his second doctorate, he learned about the work of infamous "researcher" Dr. Dan Loff.

Dazzled by the excitement and adventure, he'd announced to his family that he wanted to apply for a job on Loff's staff. His parents reluctantly agreed to let him go. But, concerned their son was going to be hired—or taken advantage of—because of his powerful last name, they'd encouraged him to adopt a pseudonym for the interview process.

"Fortune sounded cool," Gavin admitted, with a casual shrug that brushed off the terror he'd felt at the time. Everybody would surely know he was a fraud. But they hadn't, and he'd adapted quickly. For the first time, he'd discovered an advantage to being the smartest person in the room.

Brenna gave him a knowing look. "Like a comic book supervillain?"

"At the time, I was more interested in being the hero, but, yeah, that was the general idea."

"Do you think your parents were suspicious of Loff's work, even from the beginning?" Brenna asked.

"Not him specifically. The whole idea of me 'wasting my brains' on treasure hunting bothered them."

"That's parents for you—wise and judgmental at the same time."

Gavin picked up his story as he explained his work on Loff's team. Happy to be doing exciting work that had serious historical significance, Gavin had gone along with the operation for a few years. At least until he'd realized what was going on behind the scenes—collections auctioned to the highest bidder without considering their historical significance, unreported finds and disregard for family heirlooms, as Brenna had discovered with the loss of her ancestor's broach.

"It's funny," Gavin said, stroking Brenna's hand. "Loff's doctoral degree is honorary, awarded long after he'd become a successful treasure hunter. No one seems to remember that these days. He's become a myth."

"And he's done it all by hiring people smarter than him and courting the press with salacious stories and wild claims."

"Yep."

She brushed her lips across his cheek in an unexpected gesture of silent support. "So you became you by copying his model. You took the Fortune persona and rolled with it. Mystery and romance equal attention, which translates to lucrative contracts. You didn't like the way he went about his business, so you sought to steal it away."

"Did I even need to tell you what happened? You seem to have it all figured out."

"No, I didn't. And still don't, technically. But a lot of things are falling into place—your name change, your buried academic history, your dual personality, your fake playboy image."

"It's not all fake," he felt compelled to admit. "At least it wasn't in the beginning. I'd been an academic nerd all my life, and the attention I got from being a Fortune instead of a Randall, plus the press and the hot women, were seductive. My reputation in that regard isn't complete fiction."

"You wanted the spotlight, and you got it."

"Exactly. And it was great for a while."

"Until your parents realized their son had turned into a shallow, press-hoarding philanderer?

He felt his face heat. Brenna and his mother had a lot in common. "That was certainly a turning point. But when I explained why I was going through the charade—to stop Loff and others like him—they went along with my plan."

"And got a powerful judge to seal the record of your name change."

"They're supportive, but not really thrilled."

"What about news articles of you breaking up collections you've found? Ranting in the press from historical societies. Did you really do that? Are those plants? And if you told all those people—"

"Outside my parents, my agent and my crew, you're the only person who knows my real name. As for the auctioned artifacts, I buy them back."

"Anonymously," she finished before he could say it. "I found a few related stories about that happening. I always figured some crusader like me raised the money."

"That's what you were supposed to think."

She ducked her head. "I'm usually fairly smart. No genius or anything, but…well, right now I'm feeling pretty stupid."

He tipped her chin up with his index finger. "I think you're pretty great."

Bending toward her, he watched desire swim into the vivid green of her eyes. Though he was relieved she knew, he also realized their attraction had the capability to seriously complicate his already convoluted life.

At the moment, however…

Brenna pressed her lips briefly to his, but before he could deepen the kiss, she leaned back, sighing. "Then I'm really sorry to be the one to have to tell you this. Dan Loff is on Palmer's Island."

6

SHOCK REVERBERATED THROUGH Gavin's body.

He blinked. "He's here?"

"Specifically, at Mabel's." She glanced at her watch. "At least he was two hours ago."

"I—" Gavin lurched to his feet.

Would the man forever stalk him? Despite their bitter parting six years before, Loff had shown up in the middle of one of Gavin's explorations a few times. Mostly to take credit for training him and to push himself into the media spotlight. But four years ago, Gavin had told him to stop coming around and that he'd had enough of Loff's games and manipulations.

Gavin hadn't seen him since. "Did he say why he's come?"

"I didn't talk to him." She explained about seeing Loff and his media team in the diner. "I guess I freaked out. I got this weird sense of foreboding and knew I had to find you and tell you."

Gavin cupped the back of her head and gave her a quick, hard kiss. "Smart as hell."

"Yeah," she said, though she looked doubtful. "Sure I am."

She was surely taking his worries on herself, but as selfish as the dependence might be, he needed her. As well as his loyal crew. "I have to call Pablo." Using his cell phone to do just that, he warned his first mate to be on the lookout for Loff and not to leave the *Heat* until Gavin got back.

Pablo agreed without hesitation. Loyalty—another precious commodity Loff could never hope to understand or receive.

"You need to go?" Brenna asked when he disconnected, disappointment stamped on her lovely face.

"I need to *think*."

Whatever Loff's motives, they were certainly self-serving.

Probably underhanded. He wouldn't even be surprised if Loff spied on Gavin and his crew to get the exact location of the shipwreck, then snuck down there and swiped some of the treasure for himself.

He'd tried that little move on the first job Gavin had undertaken alone.

Most likely, it was simply an attempt to steal publicity. Shift the attention back to him, the supposed legend. Gavin's notoriety had to burn his arrogant ass.

All this was nothing he and his mates couldn't handle. Plus, Brenna's belief in him, her allegiance and compassion were staunch allies. Her instincts about Loff's intentions and her compulsion to warn him soothed his soul, healing the frustrated despair of the last two days.

Lost time he dearly wanted to make up for.

Watching Gavin pace, Brenna sipped from her wineglass. The powerful feelings from the lecture spilled into the moment, warming her heart. She'd been crazy about him when she thought he was a shallow, press-hoarding philanderer, hiding a mysterious past. How in the world would she save herself from falling for the academic geek, historical defender and protector?

The honor and depth she'd sensed in him weren't illusions or hopeful thinking. With the misconceptions between them gone, vanishing like smoke, she could see clearly. And she certainly liked the view.

He'd taken off his jacket when he arrived, so she was free to let her gaze wander over his broad chest, stretching the confines of his chocolate-brown T-shirt. His tanned forearms were sleekly muscled but not bulging, and she already knew the pleasure his hands and fingers could bring.

Worn jeans rode low on his lean hips, and she found herself wondering about button versus zip flies. She was pretty sure she recalled a zip the other night, but they'd stripped down pretty quickly, so she might be mistak—

Suddenly he was in front of her, bracing himself against the couch and blocking out anything but the body she'd been fantasizing about. "I certainly hope *you're* not thinking about Dan Loff."

"Well, no…not exactly." She tried to breathe shallowly so she wouldn't inhale too much of his enticing scent. They needed to figure out why Loff would suddenly show up on the island. "My attention sort of…wandered."

"Where, exactly?"

Don't look down. Don't look down.

"I, uh…" Naturally, her gaze dropped to the fly of his jeans. Were they tighter in front? Her heart pounded at the idea. "Did you come up with a reason Loff might be here?" she forced herself to ask.

"I've got a couple of ideas, though I doubt I'm putting forth my best effort at the moment."

She looked up at him and compulsively licked her lips. Heavens, he was gorgeous. "Why's that?"

Before she could blink, he'd swung her into his arms. "Guess."

He found her bedroom as if that brilliant mind of his came with its own personal GPS.

After setting her on her feet, he pulled her sundress up and over her head in one swift motion. In return, she stripped off his T-shirt. But when she laid her hands on the fly of his jeans, eager to discover the answer to her button or zip question, he stopped her.

"Hang on. There's something I want to do first."

With that announcement, he hooked his thumbs at the waistband of her panties and jerked them down her hips and legs.

With her mouth dry and her heart threatening to leap from her chest, she stepped out of them.

He braced his hands at her waist and sat on the bed, pulling her down to sit on his lap, her back to his front, her legs spread.

"Gavin?" she both breathed and questioned.

As his hands slid from her waist to the heat between her legs, he skimmed the tip of his tongue down the side of her neck. "This is all I've thought about for the last two days."

She gasped as his fingers moved in a sure and steady rhythm. "All?"

"Well, I also read a paper on the global significance and consequences of Napoleon's obsession with dominance over European nations." He flicked his finger directly over her clitoris. "Fascinating stuff. You wanna hear about it?"

Her stomach contracted; her breathing grew labored. "Maybe later."

"Whatever you want."

She could feel the heat and hardness of his erection beneath her bottom, which only made the erotic teasing more powerful. "I want you."

He dragged his mouth across her shoulder, leaving a buzz of need in his wake. "You'll have me. Indulge me a minute."

Indulge *him?*

She closed her eyes as another wave of pleasure rippled through her body. The needy coil tightened like a vise. She fisted her hands in the comforter as his strokes increased in speed.

Her climax contracted through her with gasping intensity. The aftershocks pulsed, one after the other, each one seemingly more powerful than the last. If he hadn't been clutching her against him, she would have slumped to the floor.

She'd barely caught her breath when he flicked open the front catch of her bra and pulled the straps down her shoulders. His palms cupped her breasts, his fingers dancing across her distended nipples.

And the hunger he'd satisfied roared to life again.

Turning, she straddled his hips. "Your turn."

He grinned. "If you insist…"

She laid her hand in the center of his chest and pushed him back. As he lay on the bed, she focused on his jeans.

Zip fly.

She helped him wriggle out of the denim, and as they met, skin to skin, her heart began to pound for an entirely different reason than simple lust. Touches that had started out urgent turned tender and lingering.

He seemed to take great delight in stroking her skin as he seduced her mouth with long, slow, deep kisses. She thrilled in the strength and hardness of his body. She yanked out the band holding back his hair and buried her fingers in his thick locks.

"Maybe you like long hair on men," he whispered against her cheek.

"Only on you."

They rolled, but never separated. His touch both drugged and electrified her. Getting enough seemed impossible.

With protection in place, and need overwhelming them, they came together with a gasp that was both relief and hunger. Their bodies moved in rhythmic time, their hands seeking to touch and experience every part of the other.

Brenna wrapped her legs around his hips and arched her back, straining for the completion just out of reach, though at the same time she wanted him hard inside her for hours on end.

She laid her palm against his chest, so she could feel his heart pounding, battering against his ribs just for her.

He kissed her hungrily even as his pace increased. She met him, thrust for thrust, and bit her tongue as the dam broke.

Groaning, he followed her, and she clenched her thighs around him, absorbing each and every pulse of satisfaction, glorying in the pleasure she could bring him.

Saving herself wasn't even remotely a priority.

LYING SIDE BY SIDE IN HER bed with Gavin, Brenna pressed a kiss to his warm, bare chest. With her body satisfied but still pleasantly throbbing, she decided she could really get used to this.

But duty—both his and hers—was lurking.

"Maybe you should call Pablo," she ventured reluctantly. "Isn't he waiting on you at the boat?"

He tipped her face up to his. "You're thinking about Pablo?"

Though the golden passion in his eyes remained, she could tell he was annoyed her attention was on his friend. How had he ever deceived her with his shallow-guy ruse? He hadn't been completely successful, of course. She'd always sensed something deeper in him. Or at least in them.

She'd *wanted* to believe he was a jerk. That way she wouldn't have to acknowledge how much he tempted her. How eager she was to let past disappointments go and find something, someone she could truly respect.

"Brenna?"

She trailed her lips across his jaw. "Hmm?"

"You're thinking about Pablo?"

Man, he smelled good. Gavin, not Pablo. "No."

"You're not tempted to say *'Eres el amante más impresionante del planeta'*?"

She propped herself on her forearm. "Huh?"

"You're the most amazing lover on the planet."

"How would I know if Pablo is an amazing lover?"

"I meant me."

She smiled and nibbled at his lips. "Oh, well, that's true."

Grasping her shoulders, Gavin pinned her to the mattress. "So why did you bring up Pablo?"

"Oh, right. Sorry. I got distracted again." She trailed her fingers down his chest. Maybe she was getting obsessed with that particular part of his body. "He's at the boat," she managed to say, still staring at the object of her fascination. "Waiting on you."

Hang on.

She didn't want Gavin going anywhere. "Maybe you should call him and tell him you're going to be late."

"I already called him."

She shifted her gaze to his. "When?"

"After round three and you passed out for twenty minutes."

"I didn't pass out."

"Oh, yes, you did." He kissed her cheek. "You might want to consider taking up swimming. It builds stamina."

Hang on.

"What the hell time is it?" she asked, glancing at the clock on her bedside table.

"Two in the morning," Gavin said, confirming what Brenna's disbelieving eyes were slow to register.

"Are you staying the night?"

"Depends."

Half in panic, half pleased, she wrapped her arms around his neck. "On what?"

He moved between her hips, pressing his erection at the juncture of her thighs. "Are you ready for round four?"

LYING ON HIS BACK, his body still vibrating from the last round with Brenna, Gavin let the darkness and silence of the night soothe his racing heart and troubled thoughts.

Brenna's head rested on his shoulder. Her body was cuddled to his side. Her hand lay in the center of his chest.

Dan Loff couldn't touch them.

Whatever reason his former boss had come, it didn't matter.

Gavin would find a way to thwart his plans. Hadn't he been doing that for years?

And Brenna would help him. She knew about Loff's unethical practices, just as she understood Gavin's deceptive image. She accepted his reasoning for why he'd lied. She wanted him.

That was enough. Wasn't it?

But he also knew Brenna wasn't a sidekick. She wasn't someone he could sleep with and walk away from. There were emotions between them that he'd never experienced.

For the first time in a long time, he had no idea what to do, or how to proceed. He didn't understand the parameters or scope of their relationship. His scientific brain was muddled, and trusting his heart seemed unwise.

But devotion wasn't always rational.

As history had proved, honorable men could throw themselves into fruitless causes as easily as they could noble ones.

Brenna pressed her lips against his chest. "What are you thinking about?"

"You, history and honor."

She lifted her head. "That's a very strange postcoital thought process."

"Probably." He tucked her head back against his shoulder. "You know you only gave part of Lincoln's words the other day."

"Did I?"

"'But, in a larger sense, we cannot dedicate, we cannot consecrate, we cannot hallow this ground. The brave men, living and dead, who struggled here, have consecrated it, far above our poor power to add or detract.'"

"You know the Gettysburg Address by heart?"

"Doesn't everybody?"

"And you're quoting it to me while we're naked in my bed."

"A move that might be detrimental in most relationships. But it turns you on."

"You think?"

"I do. Lincoln was saying that the sacrifice of both fighting and dying is itself a memorial. If we build a statue to the lost in every battlefield in this country, they'll still be lost. Though we should honor every soldier, they still had to fight against their brothers and leave the comfort of their homes to do so. Every life lost in a war is a tragedy. Every battle is, essentially, a failure. Where, when or how doesn't really matter."

"And sometimes a button is just a button."

He slid the tips of his fingers down her back. "Yeah."

"But when a button—or a broach—is all you have to hang on to, it becomes more than that. It becomes a symbol of sacrifice, and to not do everything we can to honor its meaning is simply wrong."

He understood her pain in a way she might never realize. He'd seen it over and over, in town after town. His sympathy was multiplied exponentially. "We're on the same side here, you know."

"In many ways, yes. But parts of what you do still disturb me."

"Me, too."

How seriously would this compromise their relationship, test the tenuous bond between them? With Dan Loff lurking in the wings, anything could happen. Usually, it was something bad.

For now, he was counting on the moonlight, plus postcoital conversation, its glow and satisfaction—anything to hold the peace. Somewhere, a clock was already ticking, and he'd be damned if his so-called brilliant mind could think of a way to halt its relentless progress.

"Why me?"

He kissed the top of her head. "I would think that would be obvious."

"I don't mean in bed." She pinched his arm. "You were serious with the history lesson. I can't be serious, too?"

"When you're serious, I'm usually in trouble."

"And you'd be wise to remember that. However, this time, for the moment, you're not." She propped herself up on her elbow and looked down at him. "I'm talking about this fake image thing, the name change, admitting your academic past. I get why your parents, agent and crew know the truth. But why me?"

Oh, boy. How much did he share here? How much did he even know himself? "I'm not sure."

"Guess."

"Because you're relentless and annoying?"

"Do you need the definition of trouble?"

"No. I have an IQ of—"

"Do you want me to sic the full force of the Palmer's Island Historical Society, including Sister Mary Katherine, on you?"

"That sounds very...unpleasant. So, no."

He could hardly deny the weight of the decision he'd made. He certainly couldn't justify his presence in her bed, his constant need for her attention, touch and respect, without answering honestly.

"Because you matter to me," he said finally, stroking her silky cheek with his thumb. "What you think—about the recovery from *The Carolina* and especially about me—matters a great deal."

She said nothing for a long moment as her clear, green eyes searched his. No doubt she was looking for sincerity. He could hardly blame her, so he held his breath the entire time.

Leaning down, she pressed her lips to his. "Thanks for that. Was it so hard?"

He wrapped his arms around her, clutching her to his chest. He was oddly anxious and relieved at the same time. "Apparently."

"If you're interested, you matter to me, too."

"I'm definitely interested, but…"

"No holding back now," she whispered.

"I've never really gotten to the relationship part of a relationship."

"The what of the what?"

"I was a geeky nerd, then I was a philanderer. There hasn't been much in-between."

"There are a lot of women buried in that confession."

"Yeah, but a lot of them were fictional."

"Just how many fictional versus real women are we talking about? At the moment, I mean."

"Jealous?"

"My last serious lover was a liar and a cheat."

"Ah. Well, I didn't— Hang on, I'm a serious lover?"

"Depends on the answer to my question."

He rolled so that he hovered over her. He liked—a whole lot—seeing her flaming hair spread in disarray across the white pillowcase. He liked the fire in her eyes even better. "I haven't touched another woman besides you since I got to the island, and I have no plans to break that pattern."

She slid her fingers through his hair. "That'll do. For now."

REALITY CRASHED WITH THE morning light.

For one, there was the light. For another, there was a loud meowing from the bathroom.

Brenna opened the door and scooped up the cat, who gave Gavin a glare before butting his head against her chin and purring like a motorboat. "You locked him in the bathroom all night?" she demanded.

Gavin—all innocence as he pulled on his jeans—said, "He kept jumping on the bed and staring at us."

Who wouldn't stare? Look at the man. He should apply for the patent on jeans and nothing else. Either Shakes was gay or had really good taste. "He's used to sleeping with me."

"You didn't do a lot of sleeping."

"I bet he didn't, either."

"I gave him a water bowl and a blanket, and his litter box is already in there. What else does he need?"

Brenna glanced in the bathroom to see the evidence of Gavin's caretaking. What man was concerned about a woman's cat?

Gavin embraced her from behind. "I don't recall you being so concerned last night."

With a hiss and a swipe, Shakes had him jumping back.

Brenna released the cat, who plopped to the floor with feline ease—even taking into account Shakes's considerable girth. She whirled to face Gavin, holding his cheek in her hand and checking for blood. "Did he get you?"

"I don't think so. You're worried about me?"

When Gavin grinned confidently, she tempered her concern with a neutral comment. Last night had been really intense, and she wasn't sure what she felt or where she stood at the moment. "Shakes can be really assertive."

"And your instinct was to protect me."

"Shouldn't I?"

"It's a pretty telling instinct."

"I never should have called you a serious lover."

"Why not? It's true, isn't it?"

"Yes, but your ego doesn't need any boosting."

"Says you," he chuckled.

She stroked his wide, bare chest. The fact that she was wearing only her robe, and her skin was one thin layer away from his skin...

"What can I do to make friends with Shakes?" Gavin asked, clearly not picking up on the direction of her thoughts.

Which was probably best. She should be ready, even eager, to see him go. After being wrapped around him for the last ten hours, she should need her space. At the very least, she should be exhausted.

She cleared her throat and tried to focus on his question. "A can of tuna couldn't hurt."

They glanced down at the cat, who was now glaring at both of them.

"How about an ahi filet from the fish market?" Gavin suggested.

"As long as you bring me one, too."

"So dinner later?"

She searched his gaze and decided that without question she liked him being so close. Even if everything else was a mess. "Yeah."

He angled his head and pressed his lips to hers. When the kiss grew heated, as their contact always seemed to do, he leaned back with a sigh of regret. "I guess I need to get to the boat."

"I'm coming with you," she said, surprising both herself and him.

"I can handle Loff by myself. He's probably looking to mooch off *The Carolina*'s publicity."

"Has he ever done that before?"

"He used to."

"When was the last time?"

"Four years ago."

Brenna lifted her eyebrows. "I'm coming."

His gaze tracked down her body. "If you come like that, you'll probably distract him to the point he'll forget why he showed up here in the first place."

"As appealing as that sounds, I think I'll get dressed."

AFTER DRESSING AND a quick breakfast of toast and fruit, Brenna drove them to the marina. "You think he'll turn up today?" she asked as she accepted Gavin's help out of the car.

"He's not here to get a tan. He's bound to find his way to the *Heat* eventually."

"What am I going to do in the meantime?"

He laid his hand in the small of her back as they headed

down the pier. "I recommend stripping off that charming dress and sunbathing on my deck."

"What about your crew?"

"I'll send them diving. Or maybe to Mars."

"What about the occupants of the boats adjacent to yours?"

"Saturn."

"What if Loff shows up?"

"Him I'll dump overboard."

"I like that plan. Is he going to hit on me?"

"Probably."

Smiling, she swung around and faced Gavin, grasping his hands as she walked backward. "If he does, are you going to punch him?"

Gavin's eyes gleamed with possession. "Probably."

"Are you going to take off your shirt first?"

Stopping, he tugged her against him. "Only if you do."

"I don't have a shirt."

He swung her into his arms and carried her across the gangplank. "Then, once again, I'm forced to suggest you strip off that charming dress."

"Forced? You're crazy. I don't see—"

"Good boy, Gavin," an unfamiliar voice interjected. "Still following in my illustrious footsteps, I see."

Gavin's hands tightened around Brenna briefly before he set her down on the boat deck a few feet away from a short, thickly built man, his dark hair liberally sprinkled with silver. Even if she hadn't recognized him from the diner, she would have known his identity by his greeting.

Condescending. Arrogant. Self-congratulatory.

Welcome aboard, Dan Loff.

Standing near Loff was Gavin's crew. They were trying to look busy, but probably sticking close to the equipment in case Loff decided either to snoop on their activities or run off with the valuables.

"Keeping pretty flexible hours, are we?" Loff asked Gavin,

though his attention was clearly on Brenna. "You're never going to find Captain Cullen's treasure like this."

A muscle along Gavin's jawline pulsed. "What do you want, Loff?"

"To be introduced to your lovely companion," he said, taking Brenna's hand and brushing his lips across the back of it.

"Brenna, Loff. Loff, Brenna," Gavin said tightly as Brenna pulled her hand away and inched out of Loff's reach.

Loff made a patronizing tsking noise. "Come on, Gavin. You can do better than that." He smiled at Brenna. "I'm Dr. Dan—"

"I know who you are," she said, before he could finish and—heaven help them—possibly recite his imaginary résumé.

"I suppose my reputation proceeds me." Loff smiled. "Understandable."

Brenna fought to keep her mouth from gaping. Part of her, though, wished she'd met Gavin and Loff at the same time. It would have saved her and Gavin a lot of time and trouble, since there was no way she would have assumed these two men were even remotely similar.

Loff turned to Gavin. "It's probably best you weren't out diving when I arrived, anyway. I have a court order to prevent you from doing so."

Gavin's gaze flicked to Pablo, who shrugged but seemed worried.

"A court order?" Brenna asked.

Loff handed Gavin a piece of paper. Her lover must have felt the same sinking sensation Brenna did, as he delayed by staring at Loff for several seconds before glancing down.

He said nothing, but the knuckles on his hand went briefly white.

Brenna tried to peer at the document. "What is it?"

Gavin said nothing for a long moment, and she slid her hand down his forearm in a gesture of support. She wasn't entirely sure he felt her touch, though. He'd gone still as a statue.

Even Shakes might lose this staring contest.

His tone wooden, Gavin finally moved enough to announce, "It seems Loff has the right to explore *The Carolina* and all its contents, since he's the ship's owner."

7

CARRYING TAKE-OUT Chinese food in a bag, Penelope walked into the Palmer's Island sheriff's office.

"Shrimp with lobster sauce?" the station receptionist, Aqua, queried as Penelope walked by her desk.

Penelope handed her the box of food. "You do know this contains lobsters of unknown origin and freshness?"

Her friend waggled her fingers. "Yeah, yeah. Gimmee."

"Where are the guys?"

"The sheriff had to go out on a call. He asked if you could put his lunch in the break room fridge."

"A serious call?"

"If you consider Mrs. Jackson claiming aliens have been bathing in her pool serious, then I suppose so."

"Again?"

"Yep. She's consistently crazy, all right. Dwayne and Finn are in the records room. Finn's still working on your project to update the computer system. Putting all the old records into the computer is taking more time than I think we expected. You know Dwayne."

"Nobody touches his filing cabinets without supervision."

"Exactly." Aqua snapped her chopsticks apart and scooped

up a bite of shrimp. She made an *mmm-mmm* noise before asking, "So, how are things between you and Finn?"

Self-conscious, Penelope shrugged. "Okay, I guess. Well, you know he took me for ice cream on Saturday night, then we went to the movies on Monday night."

Aqua's determined gaze fixed on Penelope's. "And…?"

"It was nice."

"Nice?"

"I like him." When Aqua remained fixed in her attention, Penelope cleared her throat. "A lot."

"Did he touch you?"

"Of course he touched me."

"Where?"

Penelope could feel heat invade her cheeks. "He was a perfect gentleman."

"Oh, good grief, girl. I need details. Did he kiss you?"

"Yes."

"Where?"

"On the cheek."

"Uh-oh."

Setting the bag of food on the floor, Penelope slumped against Aqua's desk. "I knew it. I screwed up somehow."

"Not necessarily. Has he called you since then?"

"Yes."

"Text?"

"Often."

"Why are you bringing all of us lunch today? Who's idea was that?"

"His."

"Hmm." Aqua ate a few more bites of her shrimp. "Okay, here's what we do."

"We?"

"I think this requires a team effort." She gestured with her chopsticks. "Take him and Dwayne their lunch. They'll want to eat in the break room."

"Why?"

"Food and Dwayne's precious records do not mix."

"Good point."

"In fifteen minutes, I'll come into the break room and tell Dwayne I need his expert OC assistance."

"OC?"

"Obsessive compulsive. Don't worry. I'll distract him. You'll have Finn all alone. Now your lunch is intimate and even has a forbidden quality—since he's at work," she added before Penelope could ask. "Finish your meal, then— What are you having?"

"Kung Pao chicken."

Aqua's eyes—heavily rimmed with black eyeliner Penelope could never pull off without looking like a hooker—gleamed. "Excellent. Rub one of the dried peppers across your bottom lip, and when his attention is caught—which it will be if you do it right—lean over and kiss him. On the mouth," she added, as if the detail was necessary—which it was.

Penelope choked. "No way. I can't. I mean, I shouldn't. I mean, I can't be that assertive."

Aqua sighed. "I'm not suggesting you push the man back on the table and have sex with him. That's for week three."

"Aqua, *please*."

Her friend grinned. "Just kidding. That's week three for me. Well, if the guy's hot and nice enough. You should go at your own pace."

"My own pace is grabbing him and kissing him?"

Aqua held up her finger. "I said nothing about grabbing. Don't grab. Just lean. I'm betting that'll do the trick."

Even as the vision of that unlikely scenario played out in her imagination, Penelope knew it was all wrong. Finn was a worldly man. She was plain ole orphan Penelope. She'd never make the right move to entice him enough to want to spend more time with her.

"Why do I need a trick at all?"

"Because you're Sister Mary Katherine's personal project," Aqua countered. "He's a man and has carnal needs, but he's holding back because of your Bambi-like innocence. He likes you—a lot—but he doesn't want to run you off. He has a shady past he's trying to overcome. He wants your trust and to woo you slowly, both out of respect and because he's probably been involved with easy-lay girls in the past. You're something else for him. Someone he respects but also wants—carnally, I mean. You need to signal to him that you're attracted to him—again, carnally—since after two dates and various other communications, I'm assuming you've already stimulated him on an intellectual basis. So you need to initiate the kiss and take your relationship to the next step."

With great effort Penelope followed Aqua's rapid-fire train of thought. There were times she'd thought her intelligence put guys off. Now, she was grateful for her brains.

And, strangely enough, she thought Aqua could be right. "You got all that from the information about ice cream, movies, kiss on the cheek, phone calls, texts and a single invitation to lunch?"

"Sure."

Penelope picked up the bag of food. "I swear I'm making it my life's work to put all these dating rules into an algorithm that can be entered into a computer, which will calculate results, revolutionize the entire process of romance, thereby providing relief and comfort to young women all over the world."

"No need. We've already got that."

"Where?"

Aqua tapped her temple. "Right here, sister."

PENELOPE SAID A SILENT prayer as she walked down the hall toward the sheriff's department's records room.

Dragging an uneatable superhot dried Asian pepper across her lips as a means to entice Finn to kiss her wasn't a remote possibility, but a kernel of wisdom existed in Aqua's advice.

Finn was holding back.

She was pretty sure she'd seen sparks of need in his eyes

when they were together, but he seemed reluctant to give in to them. How did she let him know she had similar feelings without seeming desperate—or easy?

Smile more? Smile less? Perfume? Pheromones?

Aqua got plenty of attention from guys, so maybe she was right, but Penelope was sure she couldn't pull off the pepper trick.

For one thing, the pepper itself could cause serious damage if consumed. E.R. trips came to mind.

Even rubbing the pepper across her lips would cause swelling and tingling. That seemed dangerous. Add the heat of her feelings for Finn and the carnal…whatever Aqua was determined to believe existed on his part and there was the distinct possibility of—

Oh.

Swelling. Tingling. Carnal whatevers.

She cleared her throat and glanced around. Nobody was in the hall, of course, but she could hear the guys' low voices a few feet away. Certainly neither them, nor anyone else, could know her thoughts.

And her thoughts were definitely a problem, since she was overanalyzing this whole thing way too much.

As she approached the doorway to the records room, she heard Dwayne's voice. "We are saving all the file folders, though, right?"

"Yeah," Finn said. "We'll clear some room in the basement."

"This thing could break down, and all our records would be lost."

"The system will back up every night, so we'll have a daily electronic record of everything—even if something happens to the computer."

"If you say so," Dwayne returned, sounding skeptical.

"Hi, guys," Penelope said.

Sitting at the desk in the corner of the room, Finn jerked his head up. An enticing smile pushed up one side of his mouth. "Hi."

As her heart danced in her chest, Penelope thrust the image of lips and peppers out of her mind and forced herself to move farther into the room.

Finn stood, then rounded the desk. His khaki uniform outlined his leanly muscled body and made her pulse pound even harder. After taking the bag of food from her hand, he slid his arm around her waist and pulled her against him for a hug.

Despite the fact that palm trees were the most prevalent vegetation on the island, he smelled pleasantly of woodsy pine. "Thanks for coming," he said, his breath stirring the hair at her temple.

She fought to keep breathing normally. "You guys need to eat to keep up your strength. Have to fight off that crafty Palmer's Island criminal element."

He chuckled, and she closed her eyes. Why couldn't she manage to say anything that wasn't lame in his presence?

"No eating in the records room."

Penelope glanced around Finn to the other deputy. "Hello to you, too, Dwayne."

Dwayne hooked his thumbs around his utility belt, which contained a flashlight and handcuffs but no sidearm. Dwayne was afraid of guns.

"Sorry, Penelope," he said. "It's procedure, you understand."

"Of course. Why don't we set up in the break room?"

They gathered around the large folding table in the break room. Dwayne immediately began questioning Penelope about computers. He didn't understand them, like them or trust them, which led him to lose all color when she explained about viruses and that they could infect an entire network.

"We have virus protection," Finn pointed out.

"Naturally," Penelope returned. "But new viruses are always flooding the system. He asked a direct question. I felt he deserved a direct answer."

Finn's gaze moved to hers. "But with the backups you're setting up, we'll be as secure as possible."

"The integrity of the sheriff department's records is a serious issue."

"I never said it wasn't."

"This is the most important contract I've ever undertaken. I want everything to be perfect."

"It's a computer system," Finn said. "There's no way it'll be perfect."

"Are you questioning my programming skills?"

Dwayne was squinting at her, and, worse, Finn looked upset as he leaned back in his chair.

Penelope cleared her throat. "Sorry, I'm a little on edge today."

"We have full faith in your programming skills," Finn said, still giving her a wary look.

"Thank you," Penelope said, picking up a bite of chicken with her chopsticks. She probably ought to keep her mouth as full as possible for the rest of the meal. "And the system is as safe as it can be, Dwayne. Don't worry about viruses. I'll handle everything."

True to her word, Aqua appeared in the doorway a few minutes later, begging help from Dwayne. He quickly finished his lunch, and there was a definite swagger in his step as he left the room.

"What are you having?" Finn asked her when they were alone.

Penelope glanced down at her plate. He'd probably decided food was the only safe topic with her. "Chicken."

"Is it spicy?"

"A little. Why?"

"Your face is red."

No doubt. And not only because she was thinking about dried hot peppers. "I'm sorry I snapped at you earlier."

"Forget about it. I know you know what you're doing.

I just didn't want to freak Dwayne out any more than he already is."

"And I should have considered that before I answered his questions. I could have been honest without being abrupt. I'm a bit oversensitive about my professional qualifications at times. I've found that when talking to adults—even about things I know more about than they do—I'm scrutinized for details."

Finn suddenly leaned toward her. "You're adorable."

Self-conscious, she adjusted her glasses. "I'm what?"

Then, before she could fully realize what he was about to do, he kissed her. Right on the mouth.

She gasped as he pulled back. Had that really happened? Why had it happened? She *talked* adorable? Or looked adorable?

Blinking, she watched him lick his lips. "Pretty spicy."

"It's made with dried peppers," she said, her head spinning.

"No, I mean you."

"But I wasn't even prepared." She'd planned this moment for months, and it hadn't gone at all like she'd imagined. Maybe she should have practiced more with the pillow. "I can do better," she insisted.

He raised his eyebrows. "How many guys have you kissed?"

"Including you?" She struggled for a moment between the honesty she was so committed to she'd given a speech about it, and the possibility of humiliating herself in front of the first guy who'd ever been romantically interested in her. "Two. But I think somebody dared Jimmy Mullins to do it, so that might not count."

Finn's pupils dilated.

Was that a good sign?

"You can do better, huh?" He moved his face within inches of her lips. "Show me."

Oh, boy.

She had no idea what to do with her hands, so she let them fall by her side—even though she had a brief fantasy of burying her fingers in his hair and grabbing him the way the actresses in the movies always made look so easy and hot.

He was staring at her expectantly, so she immediately closed her eyes. Before she could chicken out, she leaned forward. Her lips caught his chin, but he helpfully moved his hand to the back of her head and guided her to right spot.

His mouth was warm, but the sensation of touching some-body so intimately was foreign and a bit odd. But a spasm of excitement zipped down her spine. His piney scent enveloped her. All the fantasies of being close to him, of having him look at her like a woman and not a girl, flitted through her mind.

Tentatively, she slid her tongue across his bottom lip.

With a deep groan, he wrapped his arms around her and hauled her into his lap. His tongue explored her mouth with mind-blowing friction, yet she could still feel tension in him, as if he was holding back something much stronger.

He broke the kiss and tucked her head against his shoulder.

"I was right," she managed to say between panting breaths. "I could do better."

"Yeah, but it was perfect the first time."

"It's a forgery," Brenna said when Gavin couldn't manage to open his mouth. "It has to be."

"My claim is perfectly legitimate," Loff said, well...loftily. "What's more, Gavin's team is hereby ordered to cease and desist all excavation procedures."

"Cease and desist?" Brenna echoed, her tone climbing high with alarm. "When did *you* get a law degree?"

"He didn't," Gavin said numbly. "But he had a federal judge sign off on the injunction." He held out the paper for Brenna to inspect.

As she snatched it from his hand, Gavin shifted his gaze to Loff. The smug look on his face was infuriating. Powerless failure invaded Gavin's body with sickening speed. In an instant, he was twenty, a science geek, brilliant but knowing nothing about the world and caught in the embarrassment of intimidation and potential failure to live up to his family legacy.

He'd gone to extraordinary lengths to stop Loff's poaching. He'd sacrificed his reputation, risked his family's embarrassment, pulled his friends, crew and now his lover into his conspiracy. "Why?" was his single question.

Cocky, Loff rocked back on his heels. "I have a right to claim my property."

"*The Carolina* doesn't belong to you. It belongs to Sea Oats Shipping."

"A grievous error, my boy. One I have now rectified. As I've said, the wreckage is now mine."

"This isn't happening," Brenna whispered, looking at Gavin.

The appalled betrayal on her face made Gavin feel, if possible, even worse. All his hard work, all the compromises he'd made, the lies and blown-out-of-proportion tales.

He'd done it to make people like Brenna proud.

Now that he'd gotten close to not only her body but her hopes and dreams as well, his mission was even more critical. She mattered to him. And the community of Palmer's Island mattered to him.

Loff couldn't sweep into his life—their lives—and take away their precious history.

Gavin had to find a way to fight back. At the same time, maybe he'd earn Brenna's respect. He'd show her that the sacrifice of the lost mattered to him as much as it did her.

"Get off my boat," he said to Loff.

Shock flitted across his former employer's face. "What?"

"You heard me," Gavin said, advancing on the other man, his crew mirroring the movement as they closed in from all sides. Gavin pointed at the gangway. "Go."

Loff's tan faded instantly. "Sure thing, sport."

Brenna crossed her arms over her chest. Tiny as she was, she still managed to look intimidating. "Uh, the sheriff is a personal friend of mine, by the way, so if you want to push the issue I bet we can make sure you have overnight accommodations in Palmer's Island jail. Trespassing has a nice ring to it."

Loff pulled his mouth back in a sneer. "I'm sure the Palmer's Island sheriff is a real intimidating guy. He might even be able to outwit Barney Fife."

Brenna opened her mouth—no doubt to explain just how wrong Loff was—but Gavin moved behind her and laid his hands on her shoulders. They had nothing on Loff. Yet. "Bye, Dan."

Loff held Gavin's gaze for a moment longer, then he turned. Pablo and the guys parted to let him walk toward the gangplank. Nobody moved, or even seemed to breathe, until he'd moved down the pier and out of sight.

Brenna slumped against Gavin. "What the hell just happened?"

Pablo's attention was still directed toward the pier. "Nothing good, *cuchina*. Nothing good."

Gavin kissed the top of Brenna's head. The heady combination of the tropical scent of her shampoo and the memory of the night they'd spent together calmed him. Their bond might be temporary, but they had one.

And he needed all the allies he could get at the moment.

After all these years, he thought he'd seen all Loff's moves, all his cons and lies. And after all he'd seen and done, the places he'd journeyed, he didn't think he could be knocked off-guard like the idealist kid he'd once been. Not again.

Now Loff had upped the stakes. Considerably.

The Carolina was in jeopardy. Her treasures, her secrets and her history. Gavin's reputation and his business were on the line. As well as the admiration he so longed for from Brenna.

His book smarts would do him no good in this. Now he needed to be quick, clever and devious.

His *mentor* had taught him well, hadn't he?

"Okay, guys," he began, looking at his crew, "Dennis, I need you to go through everything we've cataloged so far. Take digital pictures of the collection and keep copies on flash drives in separate locations. Jim, go into Charleston and find some sturdy trunks with locks where we can secure it all."

Brenna glanced at him over her shoulder. "You think Loff will try to steal back what's supposedly already his?"

"It wouldn't be the first time he's resorted to direct thievery. Pablo, research the judge who signed the cease-and-desist order. Who is he, what's his record on cases like this?"

"I have a friend who's an attorney," Brenna added to Pablo. "He knows every judge in the area. I'll give you his contact information. Maybe he can get a temporary injunction from another judge to keep Loff from doing anything right away."

Gavin squeezed her shoulders. "Excellent idea. If nothing else, we'll tie things up with a little red tape."

"I'll work on the ownership of *The Carolina,*" Brenna said, turning to face Gavin. "Clearly, when you started your project, you were contracted by Sea Oats Shipping, who offered proof of their ownership, right?"

"They did. And I have all that documentation on my laptop. I'll talk to them and find out what they know. See if they've gotten the same judge's order."

"Great." Brenna moved to a deck table nearby. Setting her purse down, she rummaged through its contents. "In the meantime, you'll need help."

Confused, Gavin followed her. "I have help." He gestured at the group around them. "We've got a plan."

She was now pushing buttons on her phone. "No, I mean from the island."

"The island? The sand-based landmass beneath us is going

to animate itself and swallow Loff in a huge gulp of justifiable retribution?"

Her thumb froze on the keyboard as she glanced up. "Dr. Fortune needs to set the comic books down and join us back in the real world."

"Now *you're* talking about me in the third person."

"And I agree that's completely weird. But what I meant was you need help from the islanders. The sheriff's office, the historical society and definitely the church and Sister Mary Katherine."

"They're going to help me?"

"Sure. Well, at first it'll be me, since I've pretty much told everybody you're an amoral, grave-robbing opportunist. But after I tell them you're on our side, we'll have citizen spies, injunctions, protestors—including nuns with crosses and poster board signs—deputies with an attitude demanding proof of boating licenses and permits to operate robots in international waters, along with pretty much any other aggravation you can think of."

Gavin's head spun with her rapid-fire ideas, even as he was awed by them. "To what end?"

Brenna laid down her phone and wrapped her arms around his neck. "How much you have to learn about small-town life." She pressed a brief kiss to his mouth, which he would have liked to extend had there not been an audience and his entire career, as well as the critical history of her beloved island, at stake. "While we're proving Loff's scheme is just that, we can't let him make off with any treasures from *The Carolina,* especially Captain Cullen's legendary chest of gold—should it actually exist. So, we have to keep him from getting to the wreck site."

The gift he was being handed—not just the help with the excavation, but the trust Brenna was awarding—humbled Gavin.

He finally understood why his parents took such strong gratification from helping people. He recalled why he'd started the crusade against Loff in the first place. And it had nothing to do with money or accolades or publicity—the only things Loff cared about.

Drawing Brenna tightly against him, Gavin whispered, "You're brilliant."

"Naturally. I am the smart one in this relationship, after all."

8

"I CALL THIS ISLAND meeting to order," Sister Mary Katherine said in her gentle, but still authoritative voice.

As usual, no gavel was necessary to get the crowd to be still and quiet in their seats.

By Brenna's suggestion, they'd chosen the nun to lead the meeting rather than the mayor, as people tended to actually listen to her, and Stanley tended to tell bad golf jokes instead of focusing on the agenda. The church was also the ideal place to gather. The sanctuary was large enough to accommodate everyone, and the pews wooden and hard, fostering the necessary focus from anyone in the audience who had a short attention span. Again, the mayor came to mind.

Plus, it was Wednesday night, so the kids were available to break away from confirmation classes and serve juice and cookies to anybody who got restless.

The separation of church and state was largely a myth on Palmer's Island.

"Thank you all for coming," the Sister began, her gaze scanning the crowd with pride.

Sitting beside Gavin in the front pew, Brenna linked her hand with his. He squeezed in return, and she fought to keep her concentration on the importance of the Sister's words.

But she couldn't help but dwell on the last day and a half.

Along with his crew, she and Gavin had organized their citizen task force, who'd painted "Save *The Carolina*" protest signs by the dozens. With her lawyer friend Carr's help, they'd gotten their own injunction. The sheriff's office was on board for enforcement until the legal battles could be fought.

She and Penelope were in charge of research. Loff's claim to the ship was that he was the last and only descendant of Captain Cullen, who had, according to Loff, owned *The Carolina*. The computer ingenue was determined to break the link in this devastating fairytale.

Unfortunately, other than realizing greed was at the heart of Loff's plot, they were still in the dark about much.

The darkness, though, was where Brenna had learned the most—specifically, about Gavin's body, his various states of arousal and his capacity for satisfaction. Their compatibility in bed was unsurpassed in her life, certainly, and she had a feeling he was amazed by the strength and depth of their passion for each other, as well.

But lust didn't equal longevity. Gavin traveled the world; she was committed to Palmer's Island. Where would this thing between them go? Was it even meant to lead anywhere but to a dead end?

Her gaze bounced from her and Gavin's joined hands to the stained glass windows behind the pulpit.

Maybe she needed some juice and cookies, so she could refocus.

"As most of you know," Sister Mary Katherine continued, "the wreckage of *The Carolina,* a Civil War–era ship, was found a few weeks ago by a team of Miami researchers, who've been hired by the ship's owners to locate and excavate its legendary treasure. The recovery efforts were progressing well until Dr. Dan Loff arrived on the island two days ago, claiming the ship as his own...."

The Sister went on to explain about Loff's fishy family tree, ownership papers and his court order to stop Gavin and his crew from any more contact with the ship.

"Horsefeathers," she concluded with a decisive nod. "This Loff character is no more than a clever thief. We won't stand for this behavior on Palmer's Island, but we're going to need everyone's help to right matters again.

"Mr. Hamilton—" the Sister gestured to Carr, sitting on the other side of Brenna "—if you'd please give us a status report on the legal efforts at work."

Rising, Carr moved behind the podium. "I was able to get Judge Michaelson in the federal district court in Charleston to grant the Palmer's Island Historical Society a temporary restraining order against Dr. Loff and his team. Since Loff's cease-and-desist order was also signed by a federal district judge—albeit one out of Chicago—a ruling will have to be made by a higher court—probably the Fourth Circuit Court of Appeals, since the ship is located…" He trailed off, no doubt realizing his audience's eyes had glazed over with the first mention of a federal court. "We have the legal side tied up for the moment. No more recovery can be attempted by either side. Therefore, I need boaters and dockmaster Al to keep vigilant about the vessels that come and go out of the marina."

Al Duffy, a curmudgeon of the first order, muttered from the third pew, "Dang outsiders, stirrin' up trouble."

"That's exactly what we want to avoid," Carr said. "The sacrifice of the ship's crew and the possible cargo they were carrying are our priority. Don't approach any vessel you see violating the court orders. Radio or call in. The sheriff's department has a hotline number set up. Deputy Dwayne will tell you more about that."

Dwayne took the stage with his straight-backed stride. His face was grave and Brenna had never appreciated his precise ways more than when he recited the hotline number several times, even giving the younger people in the audience time to help the older ones enter the number into their cell phones for quick reference.

"I echo Mr. Hamilton's advice when I say the sheriff's

department has security issues firmly in hand. Report any thing strange you see, but leave law enforcement to the professionals. We've always protected our own on the island, and we'll continue to do so. Thank you for your support."

As Dwayne left the stage, the sheriffs—both the current and past one—gave him a thumbs-up.

"Protected our own?" Gavin whispered in Brenna's ear as Sister M.K. called up the president of the boater's club, who was due to encourage his members to help the sheriff's department and Coast Guard patrol the waters around the wreck site.

Brenna met Gavin's gaze. "Some of the descendants of *The Carolina* are probably still in the area."

"Probably. You don't know who?"

"Sloan's working on finding out specifics in case you guys find anything of personal value, but, no, we don't have names yet."

"All this—" he glanced around the sanctuary "—to protect unknown ancestors of people you've never met."

Not understanding whether he was confused or being critical, she shrugged. "Sure. It's an Old South thing."

He brushed his lips across her cheek. "Amazing."

"…principal research is being led by Brenna McGary and Penelope Waters. Brenna?"

At the sound of her name, Brenna jerked her attention back to the meeting. Her skin still tingled from Gavin's touch as she approached the podium, so she looked to Sister M.K. for encouragement.

The nun managed a smile of strength and peace, and Brenna was glad the Sister couldn't see inside the embarrassing turmoil of Brenna's mind. She'd pitted the entire island against a man her family had resented for generations, and asked them to put their trust in a man she'd known barely a week.

If this turned out to be a big, fat disaster, she'd be humiliated.

"Thank you all for coming," she began, trying to look

anywhere but at Gavin. His speech at the college had been so smooth and professional. She was sure she could never do so well. But, of course, she wound up looking directly at him.

And the words just came.

"The fraud Dan Loff is trying to perpetrate could have far-reaching implications to the history of our island. Men who gave their lives many years ago fighting for their principles are buried in our waters, and we're responsible for honoring and remembering their sacrifice.

"The past isn't always pretty. Often, in fact, it's bloody, hard and controversial. But we're here anyway, and all we can do is take what's offered and make the best of our legacy. We can honor those that came before us, who loved and preserved this island as much as we do.

"The team from Miami is led by Dr. Gavin Fortune, and you can place your trust in them. In him. Together, we're going to make this right."

"Would you stay with me again tonight?" Gavin asked Brenna as he pulled her car out of a space in the church parking lot.

She laid her hand on his thigh. "Love to, but Shakes won't be happy."

"What about the ahi tuna I bribed him with last night so I could have you to myself?"

"That was last night."

"How long is a cat's memory, anyway?"

"I'm not sure. Longer than a dog's, probably. Shorter than an elephant's, certainly. I'll work on that research the moment I'm done disgracing your lying, thieving, amoral former boss."

"Okay." The passion in her voice, the steadiness in her gaze as she'd given her speech in the church washed over him anew. He'd never done anything in his life to warrant so much. "I appreciate your support."

She squeezed his thigh. "My pleasure."

He'd wanted to ask her and now couldn't resist the urge any longer. Shifting the car into Park at the lot exit, he turned toward her. "Why are you trusting me?"

"Because you trusted me."

"With my identity, you mean?"

She smiled. "Among other things."

The memory of her taste, her touch, the softness of her skin and the warmth in her voice merged in a swirl of hope, wonder and uncertainty. Everything was happening so quickly. His emotions and reactions seemed stuck on fast-forward.

She cupped his cheek. "Still with me?"

The quiet of the bond between them flowed through him, slowing down his rapid-fire thoughts, pushing aside everything he didn't yet understand, encouraging him to find out what else there might be. "I could've been like Dan Loff."

"Maybe. But you're not."

"You're damn right." He linked their hands and pressed a kiss to her palm. "How about if we pick up Shakes and bring him to my place?"

She raised her eyebrows. "My bed's not comfortable?"

"It's not that. I'd just like to stick close to home right now. Well, home as in the boat."

"For you, I guess that's as homey as you get."

It had been for a long time. He didn't know anything else. His crusades were his driving force. "This project is my responsibility. And though we've got all the artifacts locked up in storage…"

"You wouldn't put anything past Loff."

"Unfortunately, no."

"Okay," she said as he put the car back in drive, "but Shakes hasn't ever been on a boat. It's entirely possible he'll freak."

"Cats have natural balance, right? Riding the waves should be a piece of cake."

"I guess we'll find out."

At Brenna's house, she packed a bag, then they grabbed the cat and fixed a fresh litter box before setting off to the marina. Shakes rode stiffly in his mistress's lap, his resentful glare fixed on Gavin the entire time.

Apparently, unlike dogs, cats did not ride well in cars.

Grateful for the marina seafood market, Gavin bought scallops for everybody and prepared to grill his way to a cozy, peaceful night.

While he set up in the kitchen, Brenna gave the feline grand tour, which didn't seem to be going too smoothly, since at one point he heard her say, "Now, Shakes, don't give me that look. I even brought your mouse."

Gavin couldn't imagine Mr. High and Mighty playing… well, anything other than a staring contest and/or head games. But Brenna's comfort level was linked to her pet's, so he was hoping for the best.

As he chopped tomatoes for a salad, he reflected that the whole scene was pretty homey. How long had it been since he'd had a real home?

His mother always said treasure hunting was his way of following the dictates of the family legacy without actual commitment to any one thing for long.

She was right. And not just because she was so rarely wrong.

He loved what he did, and considered his work a vital mission in preserving history and the integrity of maritime archeology. But his personal life was a series of meaningless hookups and temporary relationships without substance or depth. That had all been exciting and fun.

Meeting Brenna, though, had triggered something vital inside him.

Maybe his need to retire wasn't only rooted in the desire to escape the lies and the circumstances that had forced him to forsake his family name, but also to change his nomadic lifestyle, the longing to find somebody to share a future with.

Yet he'd spent so many years looking back, did he even know how to consider what lay ahead?

He was jerked from his troubling thoughts by the sight of

the cat trotting out of the bedroom with a small stuffed mouse clamped in his jaws. Gracefully, the cat leaped onto the sofa, dropped the toy, then laid his paw over it, his glowing yellow eyes daring anyone to challenge him for his prize.

After one glance at the cat, Brenna moved toward Gavin, sliding her fingers up his back and leaving a trail of heat in the wake of her touch. "A man who can cook? Is there anything on the planet that's sexier?"

He grinned. "I say we test that theory later."

She hoisted herself onto the counter, sitting beside the stove, and he handed her a glass of wine, then lifted his own. They tapped the crystal, and the result echoed through the cabin like a promise.

"Why do you keep up the Gavin Fortune persona?" she asked after taking a sip.

He coughed as he set down his glass. "There's my beat-around-the-bush girl."

"Our time together is limited, right? I don't see any point in dancing around the important issues."

Limited.

She was right, but the bald truth felt like a douse of cold water.

Though facts were his business, he wanted to reject the instincts of his scientific brain and see a romantic view of life. "I can't jeopardize current contracts," he said in answer to her question about his pseudonym.

He didn't want to go anywhere near the limited-time issue.

"Everybody would know that you're linked to a family of consummate class and charity. Plus, you have a stellar educational résumé you never disclosed, and your clients are suddenly going to run for the hills?"

Her words weren't any revelation he hadn't already considered, but doubts lingered. Some part of him was still the awkward geek, smarter than nearly everyone around him, but completely alone, too. "They hired Gavin Fortune."

"And they'd be getting Gavin Randall. An obvious trade-up."

"You don't like Fortune?"

"Of course, I—" She stopped, angling her head. "We've gone into that weird third-person area again." She snagged his arm and pulled him in front of her, where she wrapped her arms around his neck and her legs around his waist. "I'm crazy about all of you."

His erection was pressed intimately against the V of her thighs. He had trouble breathing normally. "I'm sorry. I blanked out. Are we having a serious conversation?"

She sank her teeth lightly into his earlobe, then leaned back. "Drop the Fortune thing. People generally prefer honesty over fake come-ons."

"Nobody realized my come-ons were fake till you came along."

"There's a point." She searched his gaze, and the earnest look in the depths of the Irish green overwhelmed him. "But you don't need to be somebody you're not. You don't need to live up to Loff or your family or anyone but yourself."

And you. I need your respect.

How could he be himself and risk all he'd fought so hard to protect? But if he didn't come clean would he lose Brenna's support? Would he lose her?

He kissed one cheek, then the other, then clutched her against him. "I need to get through this crisis with Loff."

That wasn't an answer, of course, but he didn't have one that would satisfy either of them.

"You owe it to yourself," she said, then released him and let him finish cooking.

Tonight there was a decent breeze and the oppressive humidity had dropped, so while Brenna laid out smashed scallops for Shakes inside, Gavin laid a blanket on deck for the humans. They sat cross-legged and facing each other, their plates and glasses between them.

Brenna complimented his culinary skills, while he tried to

keep his mind on the conversation, which was centered around the islanders who'd come to the meeting. But every time she pursed her lips around the edge of her wineglass, he wanted that mouth against him instead.

She offered to clean up, so he leaned back against one of the deck storage bins and watched the stars. After all the years of boating, he'd learned a bit about astronomy, but for the most part he liked emptying his mind and watching.

Was it as peaceful as it looked up there, or was it only quiet between battles?

When Brenna returned, he held out his hand, then tugged her into his lap. "Thanks for dinner," she said, sliding her fingers into his hair and releasing it from the band.

"Thanks for galvanizing the entire island to help me."

"I started out trying to turn them against you. I owed you one."

She had her hair pulled into a ponytail as well, so he released the golden and fiery locks to flow around her beautiful face. "But I also fed your cat, so you still owe me another one."

She smiled. "Do I?"

"Lucky for you, I have a payment plan in mind."

He shifted her legs so that she straddled him, then he wrapped his hand around the back of her neck, burying his fingers in her hair, bringing her face to his.

Sliding his tongue past her lips, he sought to seduce her slowly, savoring every touch, sigh and heartbeat.

Her silky skin was becoming a personal obsession. He grazed his lips across her cheek, then her bare shoulder. As they undressed each other, he kissed his way across every curve and plane of her body.

The vaguely tropical scent he'd first encountered he now understood was a combination of a coconut-infused shampoo and a mango-scented lotion she used daily. And he discovered familiarity was stimulating.

He'd been with many women, but he couldn't remember

ever encountering such a potent fragrance. One that brought to mind lazy beach days as well as exotic, erotic nights.

With the protection he'd stashed in his jean pocket earlier in place, he pushed her back onto the blanket and moved between her legs. She reached up with both hands and cupped his face, kissing him with sudden fierceness. His own hunger leaped.

He entered her body with her lips still on his and admitted nothing had ever been more perfect. Every part of her seemed to be wrapped and tangled with every part of him. He'd wanted to draw out every roll of their hips, but he was losing control fast.

He moved his hand down her backside, angling her for maximum pleasure. She gasped at the change, her hands clutching his back as her heartbeat went wild and her breathing turned to pants.

For a second, he felt ridiculous male pride at knowing exactly where, how and when to touch her.

Then instincts and need took over.

He pounded his way to climax, and she met him at every stroke.

She came seconds before he did, and as his own explosion overwhelmed his body, his mind was still whirling with wonder.

He might fear loneliness, but he wasn't alone. She was with him. This woman, who excited him, challenged him and needed him.

For now.

9

"CAN I CALL YOU PEN?"

Her legs swinging off the dock as she and Finn sat side by side, Penelope struggled to gauge his expression. She only had the moon overhead as a guide. "Why?"

"Finn and Pen sounds good. It's kind of cute."

"You've been convicted of grand theft auto, and you're interested in cute?"

"Yep."

"Hmm. I agree it's adorable, but I'm not crazy about Pen."

"How about Penny?"

"Why can't you just call me Penelope?"

"Everybody else calls you that. I was thinking I'd be, you know…special."

She forced herself to push past her shyness and look at him directly. "You already are."

He leaned toward her, his lips brushing hers in a light-as-air kiss that brought tears to her eyes. "I shouldn't be doing this," he whispered.

She wished he'd do it again. "Why?"

"I don't deserve you."

Surprised, she jerked back. "Huh?"

"You're revered and admired by everyone."

"You're the one who wears a badge."

He shrugged, but his pale blue eyes were hard as diamonds. "But to some I'll always be a bad seed."

"Not to me. And why do you care what anybody else thinks?"

"I don't, and you might not now, but you will someday."

"Someday? We've been going out less than a week."

"I want a future with you."

Future? Uh, until recently, she didn't even realize he'd noticed she was alive. "Finn, where is this coming from? I like being with you. And you like being with me, right?"

"Very much."

"So what—" She stopped, understanding dawning. "Who said something to you?"

"One of my buddies saw us walking on the beach Saturday night. He called me today and gave me a bunch of crap about you. You're too pure for me, stuff like that."

"And what he thinks matters to you?"

"Not really. But maybe." Clearly troubled, Finn rose. "He's right. You're sweet and smart, generous and virginal."

She glared up at him. "And there's something wrong with being a virgin?"

"No. No way."

"You wouldn't rather date some girl with more experience?"

"You're the only girl I think about." He paced the width of the dock, then crouched next to her. "You're perfect as you are. I'm the one who needs to change. I don't deserve you."

"Don't you think I should be the judge of that?"

"I'm not sweet. I'm tough. Jaded, even." He sighed. "And I'm certainly not virginal."

The idea of him being intimate with someone else made her throat tighten. And yet everything he'd been through had led him to her. Unlikely? Certainly. But as she looked at his handsome face, the concern and discomfort evident, her feelings for him only deepened. Her lustful crush became tenderness.

From there, even more lay beyond. This was a guy she could lo—

Before she could finish that scary thought, she glided her fingertips across the back of his hand, smiling when he threaded his fingers between hers. "I don't care about your past—well, except for the times you've suffered. And I definitely don't care if judgmental idiots think we're an odd couple. I'm glad you're more experienced than me. If we decide to have sex, at least you'll know what you're doing." She could feel her face heat, but she pressed on. "Our future, and our present, should be up to us."

He kissed the tip of her nose, then wrapped his arms around her and pulled her to her feet, holding her tight against him. She could feel his heart pounding intensely against her chest. "I want to deserve you."

She pressed her lips to the base of his throat. "Let it go, Finn. You can hold on to me instead," she added in a whisper.

"I'm a little overwhelmed by you."

"Me, too. Scared?"

He leaned back slightly so that their gazes met. "Not at all."

She'd questioned the other members of the historical society many times about guys and relationships. The older, wiser women had always told her that she'd know when a moment was honest, when a guy was true.

They were right.

It was perfect.

BY THE TIME SATURDAY dawned, Brenna had become part of the team aboard the *Miami Heat.*

She learned how to operate much of the equipment. She mastered cleaning the artifacts that had been found. She helped load the artifacts in secure trunks and transport them to the storage unit Gavin had rented in Charleston. She'd entertained the seemingly endless queue of reporters set up by Gavin's agent for interviews.

Yesterday, she'd navigated down the pier past the group of sign-holding protestors—Sister Mary Katherine in the lead—as a Charleston TV crew filmed a segment for the local news.

Even Shakes had assimilated to the floating office space/ housing. Pablo and the guys had accepted him like a mascot. Cats had long been thought to predict the weather, so sailors throughout history had revered them.

Brenna didn't have the heart to tell them that sneezing cats, or days cats wash behind their ears, or cats who slept with their paws tucked under were somewhat less reliable predictors than modern weather radar.

However, the fierce Friday night thunderstorm—occurring mere moments after Shakes sneezed—had caused Pablo to send Brenna a knowing look as he set a combination plate of flounder and crab for the cat's breakfast on Saturday morning.

Gavin watched the worshipful procedure with a speculative expression on his face. "Maybe you and Pablo can combine your feline-attention-span research with weather prognostication."

"Think I could get funding from the Randall Foundation?" Brenna asked.

He turned to her and grinned. "You do have an inside source for the approval process."

He kissed her, lingeringly. "I need to get out to the wreck site," he said with regret as he pulled back. "Al's taking me out under the cover of a fishing expedition, and he gets cranky when I'm late."

She curled her fingers into the soft cotton of Gavin's T-shirt, not wanting to let him go, more so because she knew fishing was the last thing on his mind. "He's always cranky."

Gavin smoothed his palm down her hair. "That's because he doesn't have a hot redhead to come home to."

He planted one last kiss on the top of her head, then moved toward the gangplank. Brenna watched him go, mostly to admire the grace and strength of his body as he moved.

It was ridiculous to be wistful. They spent nearly every minute of the day and night together. Yet she missed him when he went for dives without her. Or when she left the boat to do errands or meet with somebody on shore. At least her summer vacation from teaching hadn't been the bore she'd feared.

As any one of the historical authors she loved might say, she was well and truly besotted.

This turn in her life came down to two things, though. She was living with Gavin and no promise of a future beyond the treasure hunt existed. And they were violating a federal court order by continuing to poke around *The Carolina*.

Gavin said he was protecting artifacts from Loff, but Brenna was uneasy about his decision.

Were they righting wrongs or diving into the morally gray-bordering-on-charcoal area where Loff had lived, breathed and succeeded for decades? Gavin supposedly worried about becoming like Loff, and yet here he was, acting just like him.

Frankly, she expected either Sister Mary Katherine or Sheriff Landry to show up at any moment with indignation and arrest warrants respectively. If the nun or the cops found out they were part of an operation that was not only harassing Loff, but secretly—and illegally—exploring the wreck site, what would they do? Decide, as Gavin asserted, that they were serving the greater good?

Or condemn them for lack of ethics and betrayal?

Heading into the cabin, where she was due to meet Penelope in a few minutes, Brenna poured a soda, then sat at Gavin's desk and opened his laptop. She and the teen were deep into research-mode about how Dan Loff suddenly managed to own *The Carolina* after a 130-year hiatus.

The Sea Oats Shipping Company, who'd hired Gavin and

his team, was as baffled as they were. Though Loff had official court documents naming him as owner, SOSC had the
same thing. The whole business looked to be headed for a
long court battle, and the fate of *The Carolina* was caught in
the middle.

Basically, the crux of the matter involved two points—
Captain Cullen had actually owned his ship and not SOSC,
and Dan Loff was his direct descendent. For Loff to have a
claim, both of those facts would have to be true.

Penelope was a whiz with genealogy, so they were attempting to trace Loff's family roots. It was a monumental task,
with no clear end in sight.

When the cabin door slid open, Brenna looked over to see
Penelope entering. "I was thinking about timelines on the way
over," she said without preamble.

Brenna started to tease her about her lack of greeting. But
one look at Penelope's face stopped her. The girl was like a
dog with a bone—once she sank her teeth into a project, there
was no distracting her.

And Brenna supposed they didn't have a lot of time for
chitchat anyway.

"What timelines?" she asked as the teen sat cross-legged
on the sofa, her own computer in her lap.

"How did Dr. Loff discover he was the captain's descendant? He had to have done months of research. Look at all
the roadblocks we're hitting. The wreckage of *The Carolina*
was only found a few weeks ago. How did he get proof that
quickly?"

"He probably had a whole team of brilliant people working
on it."

"We're a team of brilliant people, and we haven't found it.
Plus, Cullen was a pirate—"

"Privateer," Brenna automatically corrected.

"Fine, privateer. He lived high and free on the seas. He
was never married—that we can find a record of, anyway.

How in the world could every one of his offspring even be recorded?"

"Maybe that's how Loff's doing it," Brenna said slowly. Penelope was onto something. "He's invented some bastard child, then linked him to the Loff line."

"Or maybe he's using his real family tree and simply claiming one of the older branches includes Cullen."

"So we have to break that link." Excitement surged through Brenna before reality crashed again. "Our problem remains the same. He's managed to convince a federal judge he's the owner. He must have offered some kind of documentation. He didn't just spin a convincing tale."

Penelope adjusted her glasses. "Naturally. That's why I asked Mr. Hamilton to see if he would have better luck getting access to the court records than I did."

"Wouldn't that involve going to Chicago?"

"It shouldn't. I called and asked for copies. Unfortunately, the court can't seem to find them."

Brenna's jaw dropped. "They've *lost* the records?"

"Apparently."

"I saw the court document Loff had," Brenna protested. "The ruling is barely a week old."

Penelope's brown eyes sparked. "Well, either somebody at the clerk's office is a complete ditz, or…"

"Or somebody lost the records on purpose." Brenna huffed in disgust. "This whole thing is fishier than Shakes's breakfast."

"And knowing that makes our job easier."

"How's that? We've been working on this genealogy for days with almost no progress."

"Well, Finn says that when you know—"

Brenna raised her eyebrows. "Finn says?"

Penelope's face reddened. "He likes to talk about his job, and I like to learn things."

Brenna hoped she was learning more than police procedure on her dates. Brenna wanted to see the sheltered teen experience life, not just read about it, and she could think of no better tutor than the cute and protective Finn Hastings. "So, you learned…"

"When you know somebody's guilty, it's much easier to prove a crime was committed."

Considering that strange circular statement, Brenna angled her head. "Huh?"

"In the courts it's innocent until proven guilty, right? But for cops, they work in reverse. They assume suspects are guilty, then test their theory against the evidence. Once they become confident somebody is guilty, then they can go about building a case against them."

"And how do they become confident in someone's guilt?"

"The usual stuff—physical evidence, alibis, witness statements." Obviously sensing Brenna's concern, she clarified, "They don't frame people to fit the facts or anything like that."

Personally, Brenna wasn't sure she was comfortable with Penelope's assessment of investigations. The fact that her lover was breaking the law even as they had this conversation probably didn't help. "If you say so."

Eager to make her point, Penelope leaned forward. "We know Loff's trying to pull a fast one and steal the treasure, right?"

"Right."

"We know what he did and why he did it. Now we need to know how. The fact that the court records are missing is the first link in the chain of proving our case."

Brenna felt a slow smile form on her face. "I like that plan. After we prove our case, can I do a back handspring on Loff's butt?"

"Sure. Can you still do a back handspring?"

Brenna tossed a wadded piece of paper at the teen. "Sure. I'm not that much older than you. It wouldn't get a ten-point-oh anymore, but—"

"He purposely took me out in that storm!"

The unfamiliar shout from the deck outside had both Brenna and Penelope rising.

"Pablo was out there when I came aboard," Penelope whispered from behind Brenna as they moved toward the door.

"He wouldn't leave without telling us." Still, Brenna's heart was pounding as she slid open the door and walked outside. The summer heat slammed against her along with a brisk Atlantic breeze.

The two women stuck close together as they headed forward on the deck. They soon realized the argument was taking place between Pablo, local fisherman Thad Raymond and Dan Loff.

"My entire crew could have been lost at sea," Loff was saying heatedly. "You people are trying to prevent me from getting to my ship, and Gavin is behind the plot! I demand to see him."

Making a serious effort to look contrite, Thad was twisting his dirty red ball cap in his hands. "I'm real sorry about the storm, Mr. Loff. Summer rains come up all of a sudden sometimes."

"It's *Dr.* Loff."

Thad squinted. "No kiddin'? You did all that studying by yourself?"

Loff cleared his throat.

Brenna bit her lip to keep from giggling. She'd given strict instructions to everyone in the anti-Loff effort to give him a hard time about his honorary doctorate. They'd caught him and his crew trying to get out to the wreck site in hired boats several times. They had to keep him away at all costs. He obviously planned to steal whatever he found.

You're doing the same thing, her conscience whispered as she swallowed a fresh lump of guilt.

"That's my treasure down there, and I have the right to—"

"*The Carolina*'s ownership is still under debate," Pablo

said firmly to Loff. "Nobody is supposed to be exploring the site."

Brenna suppressed a guilty wince. All she needed was for her friend, who was both highly intelligent and dating a cop, to get wise to the real nature of Gavin's "fishing expeditions." So far, only she and Gavin's crew knew Gavin was still retrieving artifacts from the shipwreck in order to protect them from Loff.

Loff noticed Brenna and pointed at her. "You put him up to it."

Brenna crossed her arms over her chest and cocked her hip. "Gee, Dan, I have no idea what you're talking about."

"You think Brenna controls the weather?" Pablo asked, his tone disbelieving.

"I think he means I'm the brains behind Dr. Fortune's operation," Brenna explained.

Loff looked amused. "Not the brains certainly." His eyes narrowed. "But the instigator. In addition, I'm certain each and every one of you would like to see me at the bottom of the Atlantic, along with my ship, and you deliberately sent me out with this incompetent idiot, knowing there would be a storm."

"Don't you dare call him names. Thad's the best fisherman on this island," Penelope said fiercely, fisting her hand at her side as if she was restraining the urge to punch Loff.

And weren't they all?

Correct as his assessment was.

"But you weren't interested in fishing, anyway, were you?" Brenna commented, deliberately putting insult and suspicion in her tone. It was either that or fold beneath the pressure. They were beating Loff at his own game.

Didn't they *have* to? Didn't she and her family deserve to see Loff suffer as much as anybody?

But the idea of Gavin and this creep using the same ploy made her nauseous. How long could they expect to get away with their deception, righteous as it might be?

"What else would I be doing?" Loff returned, pompous indignation oozing from every pore. "I need something to pass the time while I wait for my property to be rightfully awarded to me."

The way Loff twisted facts to suit himself was both amazing and appalling. Self-centered was a serious understatement with this guy. "You're the one who hired Thad to take you out in his boat," Brenna said. "If you weren't comfortable with his qualifications, then I'd say that's your problem." As she paused for breath, she considered something important. "What did you need him for, anyway? Where's your boat?"

"It's being brought down from Maryland. I knew I needed to get here right away to assert my claim on the precious cargo of *The Carolina*. While I was waiting, I decided to do some fishing and I only hired Thad because your harbormaster recommended him."

It was a logical story. One Brenna didn't believe a word of.

"He agreed to take me out on my fishing expedition—right into a fierce thunderstorm," Loff continued. "He did so on purpose. I ought to file harassment charges."

"That's some case of paranoia you've got there, Dan," Brenna said condescendingly. The memory of Shakes's sneeze crossed her mind, but she could hardly be expected to consider that a legitimate storm warning.

"Doc Lambert helped a buddy of mine when he kept dreamin' about giant catfish," Thad interjected. "I could give you his number."

What would they do without Thad—or any of the generous islanders who'd given their time and effort to make trouble for Loff? The togetherness made the anxiety of Gavin's precarious situation manageable.

Al and the local fishermen were especially helpful in the covert operations. They took her, Gavin and his crew out on their boats under the guise of checking crab traps or trolling for flounder. Though they undoubtedly suspected what was actually going on, no one had said a word.

"Don't worry, Loff," Pablo said, suppressing a laugh. "We'll watch over the wreck site while you get therapy for your various psychological issues."

"Where is Gavin?" Loff demanded.

"Out," Pablo said easily. "He has a variety of media and client obligations. He's not blessed with a schedule that allows him to…fish for hours on end."

Pablo obviously knew Loff well enough that the media dig would get to him. And it did. Loff's face was nearly crimson as he shoved his hands into his pants pockets. "So he leaves his second-best and the ladies in charge." Loff smirked. "How generous of him."

"He trusts us," Brenna returned, her blood on the verge of boiling. "A concept you'll never understand."

"My dear," Loff began, taking a step toward Brenna with both malice and interest in his eyes. "You can't possibly—"

Pablo darted between them. "We're a pretty easygoing group, Doc, but you might consider taking your temper elsewhere."

Loff let his cold gaze linger on Brenna's another moment before he turned. "Oh, I definitely will."

As he walked away, Brenna breathed a sigh of relief. The encounter was bad, but her own guilt certainly made everything more pronounced. She wasn't sure how much more of this she could take.

Loff stopped suddenly and stared over his shoulder directly at her. "I'd like to speak with Brenna alone for a moment."

Pablo simply shook his head. "No way."

"It's rather personal," Loff said. "I imagine she wouldn't want this conversation overheard by everyone."

Personal? What was he going to do—make another cheap pass? Frankly, she'd rather have witnesses for that. "What is it?"

With a confident expression on his face that Brenna didn't

like at all, Loff closed the distance between them. "Gavin has a special skill with charming locals. He's learned charisma from an expert—and of course he has that pretty face."

Brenna accepted the jab about being one of the varied and many *locals*. But she also understood Loff's weakness. "He's certainly gorgeous." She deliberately let her gaze rove his mildly-attractive, but unremarkable face. "Surely you don't think you're the charming expert?"

Rather than recognizing the derision, he chose to sink further into his King-of-the-Castle delusion. "But I am." He winked.

"Gavin also has an extremely short attention span when it comes to intimate encounters. In a few weeks, he'll move on to another hot, young…" He paused, scanning her from head to toe. "Perhaps an even hotter and younger woman."

Penelope gasped.

Brenna and Loff ignored her and continued to stare at each other.

"You'll be left with a broken heart, while he sails off to his next adventure." Loff's smile was patronizing. "Are you sure you want to protect him?"

"You bet I do." Brenna's smile was fierce. "If he needed it. He doesn't. You do." She lowered her voice to a whispering threat. "I have my own, very personal reasons for standing against you, and they have nothing whatsoever to do with Gavin. Your thieving past is about to come back and choke you, Mr. Loff."

The sound of hurried footsteps echoed down the gangplank. "I heard shouting."

Brenna spared the newcomer a glance, noticing Dwayne was out of breath and sweating. He even had a gun in his hand. Bless his heart. It probably wasn't loaded, but the sentiment was touching all the same.

"Everything's fine, Deputy," Brenna said, shifting her gaze back to Loff. "Dan was just leaving."

With a jerky nod, even though his eyes spoke to his fury, Loff did just that.

Once he was gone, Dwayne demanded an explanation, so Brenna gave him a brief rundown.

"I want to know how Loff got to us without a warning," Pablo said when she was finished. "I turned around, and he was nearly on board. Who's supposed to be watching him today?"

"It was Al's shift," Thad said. "But he had to help a tourist tie off his boat, so he asked me to look out. I saw Mr. Loff headin' this way, so I followed him." He grinned. "Sounds like I'm one of the ones he wanted to talk to, anyway."

"*Did* you know there would be a storm?" Penelope asked.

"I figured there might be," Thad admitted. "But don't worry, I can handle myself. I'm not so sure about Mr. Loff, though."

Brenna laid her hand on the fisherman's arm. "We appreciate your help, Thad, but please don't risk yourself or your boat on account of us."

"Did you by any chance see a cat sneeze yesterday?" Pablo asked after a brief look in Brenna's direction.

Thad shook his head. "Nah. I got weather radar on my boat."

Brenna smiled knowingly at Pablo.

Of course, the smile faded when Thad added, "But a sneezin' cat's a surefire warnin' sign, I'll grant ya."

Brenna sighed. "Oh, good grief."

"ARE YOU IN LOVE WITH Dr. Fortune?"

Brenna choked on her soda. "You gotta warn a girl before you ask questions like that, Penelope."

The teen handed her a napkin. "Sorry. I know it's a personal question."

"Is there a reason you asked it?"

"Is there a reason you don't want to answer it?"

"I don't know."

"The answer or the reason?"

Despite the confusion swirling deep inside, Brenna smiled "The answer."

They were supposed to be working on finding Loff's genuine family tree, so they could compare it to the fake one he'd probably given to the court to prove his ownership claims. But without much to show for their efforts, they'd taken a snack break, leading to Penelope's personal inquiry.

"Have you ever been in love?" Penelope asked.

"I thought I was once, but things didn't work out." And, really, the feelings she'd had for her ex didn't remotely approach the intensity of what she felt for Gavin. So what did that mean? Had she loved the ex and lusted for Gavin, or the other way around?

Or neither?

Penelope set down her water bottle with a snap. "Well, then, how are you supposed to tell me if I am?"

Startled, Brenna glanced at her. "You are what?"

"In love."

"Oh." This wasn't about Brenna and Gavin, but Penelope and Finn. The distress on the younger woman's face penetrated Brenna's egocentric thoughts. "Oh, sorry."

Not sure how to proceed except to tell her own story, then listen to Penelope's, Brenna crossed to the sofa and sat beside the teen. "I'm not exactly an expert source in this area. I spent elementary school, middle school, high school and most of college training. I was in the gym thirty hours a week. If I hadn't messed up my knee, I probably wouldn't have graduated, because all I cared about was gymnastics.

"I dated a little when I moved to Atlanta and got my first job, then this really hot guy noticed me at a party. He talked to me and complimented me, and I fell hard. We moved in together, and I thought I loved him and that he felt the same."

"But...?" Penelope pressed.

"I came home from work early one day and found him in bed with one of the girls from the cleaning service."

"Yikes."

"It wasn't fun." Brenna shrugged off the pain that had been so prevalent until recently. "But I moved back to the island, reconnected with old friends, got a great job I love and even began dating again." She gave Penelope a wry smile. "Though without much success."

"Then Dr. Fortune arrived on the island."

"He pretty much blew in like a summer storm. We disagreed, we argued our points, we found a middle ground, we…"

"Can't take your eyes off each other."

Or our hands. Brenna nodded. "Pretty much. What about you?"

"Well, I…" Penelope twisted her hands in her lap. "I've spent my entire life studying, and I think I've fallen hard for a hot guy who suddenly noticed me."

This last rush of information had Brenna biting back a curse. She should have listened first. How many coaches had told her she was too aggressive on the mat and that she needed to think before she—literally—leaped?

Brenna cleared her throat. "First off, Finn isn't my ex."

"But you don't know he's not like that," Penelope returned fiercely.

"No, I don't. And neither do you. Relationships are a gamble. No guarantees. But there are some things to look out for."

Penelope's face brightened. "Okay, good. Rules. I like rules."

Wow, she was probably in over her head. But Penelope was Brenna's friend, and deserved her candor. "I don't know if these are rules per se. Certainly not universal ones. But I guess they're sort of my personal guidelines."

Still seeming eager, Penelope nodded. "Okay."

"Does he treat you with respect?"

"Definitely."

Frankly, Brenna hadn't expected anything less from Finn but her ex had been respectful in the beginning. He'd still cheated. "Does he listen to you?"

"Sure. We argue sometimes, though."

"About?"

"Virus protection."

Brenna coughed. Penelope and Finn were having sex? Oh wow, she was really drowning here. "Like STDs?"

Penelope's face went white. "No. *Computer* viruses. I haven't—I mean, we haven't—"

Brenna waved her hand. "It's fine. Good. There's no need to rush things. You have plenty of time for intimacy. And back to my original point, you don't have to agree all the time. Debate is good. Standing up for yourself and your opinions is even better."

"Oh, I definitely do that."

"Great. So even if there's no sex involved, and I see no reason for a rush in that regard, does he still…" How did she put this to a nun's protégée? "…uh, rev your motor?"

Penelope looked confused for a moment. "You mean, am I attracted to him physically?" When Brenna nodded, she said again, "Definitely."

"And he to you?"

"We made out in the sheriff's office break room the other day, so I guess so."

"Has he ever given you a reason to doubt he cares about you as much as you do him?"

"No."

The immediate answer made Brenna smile, so Penelope gave her a searching look.

"Did your cheating ex give you doubts?" she asked.

"Yes. Part of me always knew I was way more into him than he was into me."

"I don't feel like that with Finn. I feel…cherished. Is that weird?"

"No." Brenna grabbed the teen's hand. "Good. That's wonderful."

"He says he wants a future with me. But it's all happened so fast, and he's worried he's not good enough for me."

"Why?"

"The prison thing."

"Are you worried about that?"

"Not at all."

"If it helps, I see him look at you, and I see a guy who's really, really interested."

"Does that mean I'm in love? Or he's in love?"

"Is he the most important person in your life?"

"I think so." Penelope stared out the window, as if looking for guidance beyond this world. "Yes."

Brenna squeezed her hand. "So enjoy it. Don't think so hard."

"Is that what you're doing?"

"I'm trying. It's easier for me, though. I'm not as brilliant as—"

She stopped as the cabin door slid open and Gavin walked in.

He wore an olive-green T-shirt and rumpled cargo shorts, and he'd never looked more gorgeous. Brenna's heart rate picked up speed even before he saw her and smiled.

Then her heart simply melted.

Crossing to her, he placed a brief kiss to her forehead. "How's the research going?"

"Lousy."

"Not possible." He kissed her cheek as if one hadn't been enough. It never was for Brenna, either. "Not with you two beautiful ladies working on the case."

"Well, neither beauty, nor apparently brains, is working."

"We need to think like a cheat," Penelope added.

"Ah." Gavin straightened. "Both of you are pretty straight shooters, so that's going to be a problem. I've been known to have a few devious ideas. I'll take a shower, and we can talk about it over dinner, okay?"

Personally, Brenna was more interested in using her mouth for something besides eating and talking. But with Penelope present, she could hardly indulge that desire.

She watched Gavin walk away until he disappeared down the hall. *Oh, my.*

"Um, I think I'll be going," Penelope said, closing her laptop.

Brenna dragged her gaze back to her friend. "You don't have to go."

"Actually, I do. I'm meeting Finn for dinner." Penelope grinned. "I think you and Dr. Fortune could brainstorm better without me."

Rising, Brenna hugged the teen, then walked with her onto the deck. She made sure Pablo escorted her to her car, which he was happy to do, since he was heading out, as well.

Back inside, she started throwing together a simple dinner of spaghetti and salad.

She was glad Penelope and Finn had found each other, though one thing Brenna didn't share with the teen was the worry and fear that even if she was the most important person in someone's life, she might not be the highest priority.

Gavin cared for her, but his dedication to his hunts was absolute. He'd given up his very identity to keep them viable.

Loff might have been mean, but he was right about one thing. Eventually, Gavin would move on to the next adventure. Not because he was desperate to leave her, but because the sea—and his hunts, by extension—was his first and only love.

She could hardly compete with that.

And even if she could, she didn't see how they could last. He seemed to have no problem breaking the court order as long as he found the treasure. He said he wanted to protect the artifacts from Loff, but she wondered if it was safeguarding history or beating his old boss that was more important.

She wanted to beat Loff herself, but at what cost? Wasn't it enough that they spied on and followed him 24/7, keeping him from stealing the treasure? Even though Loff's ownership papers had to be fraudulent, shouldn't they, too, be bound by the law until the truth was discovered?

Could she be falling for a man whose integrity was on shaky ground?

The worry about his true motivation tightened her stomach as she stirred the marinara sauce.

Should she ask him? Did he even know?

Minutes later, he joined her at the stove, sliding his arms around her from behind. He pressed his mouth to a stimulating spot behind her ear. "Mmm. Something smells good."

"It's only jarred sauce with fresh basil added."

He slid his lips down the side of her neck. "I meant you."

Need roared low in her belly. She couldn't imagine a day without that feeling. A day when he'd be gone. Turning, she looped her arms around him. She absorbed his now-familiar combination of soap and woody citrus cologne. "Same goes, Doc."

He leaned down and kissed her.

Belying the easy moment, she clutched him to her. The kiss became heated.

When they parted, they both struggled to catch their breath. The golden flecks in his hazel eyes were bright with heat.

"Let's eat fast," he suggested.

10

HIS HEART THREATENING TO vault from his chest, Gavin flopped to his back on the bed beside Brenna. "Are you sure you didn't put something else in the sauce besides basil?"

"Like what?"

"Some kind of super fruit? An herbal energy supplement? Hummingbird food?"

With a laugh, she rolled on top of him. "You're enough of a supplement."

Weakly, he glided his hand down her bare back. "If you say so."

She laid her head on his chest and hooked one of her legs around his, as if trying to hold him in place.

Though he wasn't going anywhere, he found the clinging odd. Even her lovemaking had an extra edge tonight, as if she were desperate to touch every part of him at the same time. She seemed more than passionate, bordering on anxious.

"Is everything okay?"

She didn't relax her hold on him. "Sure."

Feeling the tension in her body, he stroked his fingers up and down her back, hoping to soothe whatever was affecting her. "Are you worried about Loff?"

"Some."

"We can handle him. You and Penelope will find something

to prove he's a fraud. And isn't your attorney friend, Carr, working on some legal maneuvers?"

"He is, but Loff could still tie up *The Carolina*'s treasure in courts for years."

"Which is why we're continuing explorations in secret. At least the artifacts will be protected instead of continuing to rot on the ocean floor."

"But eventually somebody will know you kept excavating past the date of the cease-and-desist order. Don't you catalog all the finds?"

"We'll backdate them."

Her body jolted, then she sat up. "Isn't that the kind of thing Loff does?"

"Yes, but he does it to swindle people. We're doing it to protect a valuable part of history. *Your* history. We can't sit around waiting while the lawyers and judges battle."

"Right!" She rolled off the bed, snatched a sweatshirt off the dresser, then pulled it over her head. "You have other clients waiting on you."

And there it was—the elephant in the room. His eventual departure from the island. He sat up and extended his hand toward her. "Come here."

She looked at him a long moment before she complied. Then, her hand linked with his, he stared into her eyes. "I'm not going anywhere for a while."

"But you are going."

He wanted to make promises, but didn't see how he could. "I have contracts to fulfill."

"I know." She leaned down and kissed him gently. "I'm sorry. I shouldn't have brought it up."

Gavin hated the resignation in her tone. "Come back to bed."

"I will. I'm only getting a glass of water."

He clung to her hand. "Are you upset with the way I'm handling *The Carolina?*"

She shrugged. "It's a complicated situation."

"Whatever the court decides I'll comply with."

"Like you're complying now?"

A spasm of pain seized him.

She must have sensed his hurt, because she squeezed his hand. "Sorry again. It's just difficult for me. I don't know what to think."

She obviously needed a minute alone. Maybe he did, too. He let her go.

When she left the room, he lay back on the bed.

He wanted her admiration and respect for his job as much as he craved her body and her touch. But sometimes a fair fight wasn't possible.

Though he had to admit he hadn't counted on drawing half the island into the conspiracy.

He hadn't told Thad, Al or any of the other fishermen helping him that he was bringing up relics from the wreck. So far they'd all been small enough to conceal in a pack attached to his diving suit. He'd even managed to convince Penelope that he and the crew were only watching out for Loff, not actually bringing up treasure.

But did the team suspect? Did their inadvertent assistance constitute violating the court order?

Shakes leaped onto the bed, parking himself in the center of Gavin's chest. The cat stared down at him with a hard expression, as if agreeing with his self-directed criticism.

"I don't need that look from you, too, buddy," Gavin said, nevertheless scratching the cat between his ears.

Shakes graciously, but briefly, accepted the strokes, then stuck his nose in the air and slunk to the end of the bed, where he turned his back and stared in the direction of the bedroom doorway. No doubt waiting for Brenna's return.

"Great." Gavin pulled a pillow over his face. "Everybody's mad at me."

"I'm not mad at you," he heard Brenna say.

"Disappointed, then," he muttered into the pillow.

He felt the bed dip as she sat beside him. She tugged the

pillow, and he reluctantly tucked it behind his head. Seeing the worry in her eyes made him feel like a jerk.

"I'm concerned," she said, leaning over him. "And confused. I know the world isn't black and white. I accept shades of gray. I'm thrilled sweet and innocent Penelope is dating an ex-con, for one. But I feel like since Loff showed up things are turning green and purple and every other color in between."

"The alternative is letting Loff get his hands on the artifacts. Are you willing to let that happen?"

She seemed to struggle with her answer. "I don't know."

"Well, I'm not."

"No matter the cost?"

"It's my job to—"

"Come on, Gavin. This stopped being a job the moment Loff showed up. You're on a crusade now."

A spark of anger ignited. "And what's wrong with that? When we first met, and you thought I was like Loff, you were hell-bent on stopping me from getting my hands on that ship."

"And everybody around me was concerned I was taking my mission too seriously."

"Not me. I see nothing wrong with determination, fighting for what you believe in. It's one of the traits that first attracted me to you."

"Any means to the end we want?"

"Not any means." He looked away, sighed, then shifted his gaze back. "There are lines I won't cross. I won't be Loff."

"I know. But in the end all we have are our principles, our reputation and our history." She traced his jawline with the pad of her thumb. "And our freedom. Have you considered that if somebody learns you're bringing up treasure, you could be arrested? The sheriff's a sharp guy. He has to suspect you're doing more than watching over the wreck site. He can't look the other way for long."

"I don't care."

And, yes, it was disappointment that crossed her face.

As she leaned back, he sat up. "To clarify…I don't care what happens to *me*—as long as I stop Loff in the process. What kind of man am I if I can't protect what matters to me?"

The vivid green of her eyes stood out from her pale face. "Do you want to protect the treasure, or do you want to win?"

"What the hell—"

A pounding on the cabin door halted his question. Probably best, since he might have said something he'd regret later.

With hurried, jerky movements he put on his jeans and stalked from the room. "Stay here."

Naturally, she ignored him and followed him down the hall. "You're not exactly dressed for company," he pointed out.

"Neither are you."

Gavin was relieved to see Pablo through the glass door. After flicking open the lock, he let his colleague inside. "What's wrong?"

"That sneaky jerk's done it again, *amigos,*" Pablo said, waving a piece of paper. "Loff's got himself some free— if completely fabricated—publicity courtesy of the island newspaper, and he's throwing a big party Monday night to celebrate."

Gavin snatched the paper. "Celebrate what?"

Pablo's smile was jaded. "Himself naturally."

"Who wrote the article?" Brenna asked, peeking around Gavin's shoulder.

"Some guy named Jerry Mescle," Pablo said. "Know him?"

Brenna groaned. "Unfortunately, yes."

"IN THE WORDS OF THE estimable Sister Mary Katherine, this is a crock of bull."

Standing beside Brenna on the town hall steps, Gavin raised his eyebrows. "Nuns say 'crock of bull?'"

Brenna waved her hand. "In the vernacular."

Gavin surveyed the party scene in front of them. "He's certainly gone all out."

"Humph" was all Brenna could bring herself to say. To sway public support in his favor, Loff had splurged for a come-one, come-all barbeque, with all the fixings.

Thanks to Pablo's spy at *The Herald,* resulting in the early peek at Jerry Mescle's article that had been plastered across the Sunday morning paper, Brenna had been able to assemble the anti-Loff forces to infiltrate the party. Loff had challenged the Sea Oats Shipping company—Gavin's employers—for ownership of *The Carolina* for everyone to read, and they needed to know how the public debate would affect them. The results could be as important as the looming court battle.

Not that Loff or anyone else would notice their citizens' brigade.

Free food and beer had brought out the masses. Amid red, white and blue decorative streamers and balloon clusters, they milled around the town hall grounds, the brightly blooming gardens and the brick path surrounding the statue of General Beauregard Palmer.

Even in the oppressively sticky June heat.

The shops along the square were doing a brisk business. The kids' craft tents were overflowing with all ages, from toddlers to middle schoolers. And everybody Brenna saw held cups of beer or lemonade and plates of barbecue and potato salad—all looked as happy as clams in wet sand.

Traitors.

She was trying to save their island from moochers like Loff, and they were standing in line to be grill on a spit.

The fairly silent pseudo-bribe party Loff had pulled off would have nudged her into admiration—if she wasn't sure his intentions were absolutely selfish and to the detriment of her hometown.

While the task force had been watching Loff around the marina and his hotel, a member of their amoral rival's staff had been schmoozing the island's Powers That Be. Much to the sheriff's annoyance, the mayor had signed off on a permit for the whole shebang after a meeting with Loff's lackey Saturday afternoon, while Loff had been aboard the *Heat* distracting Brenna and the crew.

No telling what Stanley—the mayor—had been promised, though Brenna intended to make it her personal crusade to find out.

Golf clubs, no doubt, had changed hands.

Adding this public relations fiasco to the tension between her and Gavin and the certainty that their time together was careening to an end, she was understandably edgy, frustrated and furious.

"This is my fault," she blurted out, watching with narrow eyes, as, in the distance, Stanley demonstrated his golf swing for a group of Bermuda-shorts-clad men.

Gavin shoved his hands in the pockets of his cargo shorts. "It's mine. Loff's an expert at manipulating people and publicity. I know that better than anybody."

"I should have had somebody watching Stanley 24/7. He was always our weak link."

"He's the mayor. He can't deny happiness to his constituents. Instead of doing an interview for a national magazine like *World Adventure* this week, I should have gone to the local newspaper and offered to tell them some of my stories. I should be hanging out with the islanders, building excitement for the historical treasures we're going to find." He sighed, deeply. "I usually do."

Pressure settled heavily on Brenna's chest. "Instead, you've been with me."

Gavin's gaze jumped to hers. A world of confusion lived within the hazel depths. She'd once questioned the motivations for his job, and now she was affecting the way he did it. Heaven knew Gavin was smart enough to handle both, and yet she couldn't dismiss the similarities between him and his former boss. Without question—at least in her mind—they were there.

Pablo moved between them. "You two need to pull it together. The pictures we've gotten this week from *The Carolina* are the best yet. We're going to find that chest, and when we do, all this—" he gestured to the frivolity around them "—won't mean crap."

"How can you be so calm?" Gavin returned, his eyes dark and boiling. "Loff has an article in the paper about how he's protecting the island's history despite my *fumbling, amateurish* attempts to taint it. He's claiming he'll build a museum displaying the artifacts, increase tourism and, hang on, wait for it…honor the fallen." He flung his arm toward the gathered crowd. "I know for a fact that he won't do a damn thing, and now he's giving away free food!"

"Bribe," Brenna asserted.

"Smoke," Pablo argued. "He's distracting everyone from the crux of the issue—namely, he's trying to steal the damn treasure from under the town's nose. Don't let his name-calling sidetrack you from the real issue. He's here for him, no one else."

"Pablo's right." Brenna snagged Gavin's hand. Despite, or maybe because of, their argument, she couldn't bear to see his anguish. "We use the party to counteract Loff's plans. We expose his lies."

"How?" Gavin countered harshly.

"Go find another reporter and offer to give him an exclusive interview." She snapped her fingers as an idea hit her. "There's a new girl—Sasha. She's a senior at The College of Charleston. Smart, but inexperienced. Jerry rags her about doing the 'fluff' pieces, while he gets all the big stories."

She scanned the area for the young woman she'd met at the hair salon at the beginning of the summer. Miraculously, she spotted her among the crowds. "There, by the kids' face-painting tent."

A ghost of a smile teased Gavin's mouth. "I like it."

"Plus, it'll burn Jerry's ass. Stay away from him, by the way. He'll just piss you off." Brenna pointed in the direction of the beer tent. "Jerry's the smarmy one standing next to the guy in the polyester suit."

"Polyester in June?" Gavin asked in disbelief.

"Polyester in this decade?" Pablo wanted to know.

Brenna gave a critical shake of her head. "His cousin, Clyde, is an island unto his own in regards to fashion."

"What are you going to do?" Pablo asked Brenna.

"Find Sloan. I set her and her husband, Aidan, the task of following Loff around. They're probably ready to kill him by now."

"Solving all our problems," Gavin said, anger lingering in his eyes.

His seething disposition, which he'd sunk into all day yesterday, seemed destined to worsen. She wanted her charming lover back.

However long she could keep him.

Brenna rose on her tiptoes and brushed her lips across his stubbled cheek. "We'll fix this. Don't worry."

Leaving him, she headed down the steps and into the crowd. Loff and his video crew shouldn't be hard to find. Especially since she'd already spotted him wearing a neon green polo shirt.

She found him and his group, plus Sloan, near the statue of General Palmer. With the videocamera rolling on the scene, a few locals stood by their faces wreathed in awe as they snapped photos. Two men Brenna didn't recognize flanked Loff. One held a small duffel bag; the other publicity stills and pens. Both looked at their boss as if he were responsible for the rising sun.

Briefly, Brenna closed her eyes. Surely that sickly devoted expression had never appeared on Gavin's face. No matter how young and idealistic he'd been when he'd worked for Loff.

While Loff was busy talking to the locals about his favorite subject—himself—Brenna approached Sloan, snagging the sleeve of her shirt. "What's happening?"

Sloan flipped her long blond hair over her shoulder with a

huff. "He's made so many passes at me, he ought to be in the NFL. Aidan was with me earlier, but I had to send him off to get a beer. I was afraid he'd punch the guy out."

"Resulting in yet even more sympathetic publicity for him."

"Exactly."

Sloan had no doubt made the right move regarding her husband. Beneath his sophisticated veneer, Aidan was all alpha male. "Who're the video guys?"

"They're from some cable show, supposedly doing a documentary on Loff."

Brenna's heart lurched. If anybody deserved credit for finding the wreck site, it was Gavin. "About *The Carolina?*"

"About Dan the Magnificent."

"Just what the home viewer needs. Have you seen anybody else from our side?"

"Al and a few fishermen are around somewhere. I told them to keep their ears open for what the islanders are saying about Loff—do they believe him or Gavin, that kind of thing. Sister M.K. and some of the other nuns have walked by a couple of times. They stare holes through Loff that would have me running to the nearest church pew to beg for mercy, but he smiles and nods. Amoral is an understatement with this guy."

"Tell me about it."

"Penelope and Carr are in Gilda's bakery using the WiFi," Sloan continued. "Both in deep research mode. According to them, no matter how this PR nightmare damages us, the courthouse is where the battle will be won. And the sheriff and his team are working."

Unfortunately, because of the very legal permit Loff had gotten from the mayor's office, Tyler, Finn and Dwayne were all forced to help with the party, supervising crowd control and directing traffic.

"Why, Miss McGary, how nice of you to attend my little soirée."

Responding to Loff's fake, ingratiating voice, Brenna

stiffened. "How could I resist? Keeping tabs on you has sort of become a hobby."

Loff's smile exploded with pleasure. "You're welcome to watch me as closely as you like. My former apprentice tends to get, well, distracted easily. But my focus is absolute." His muddy gray eyes were bright with invitation.

Brenna barely resisted the urge to say something nasty.

Sloan saved her by grabbing her arm. "We really need to…"

Take a break from standing near you, Brenna thought.

"Go," Sloan finished. When they were out of earshot, she added, "Yuck."

Brenna nodded. "Amen, sister."

For the next couple of hours, she and Sloan kept an eye on Loff, but from a distance. Quite a few islanders approached Loff for autographs and pictures, but others watched him suspiciously.

After nearly two hours, Brenna was sweaty and annoyed. She wanted a cool shower. And Gavin. As expected, every minute of the day, she wanted Gavin.

Obviously sensing her friend's state, Sloan retreated to the lemonade tent for two glasses. Handing Brenna one, she toasted her. "Might as well drink on Loff's dime."

Brenna took a sip, but the taste made her nauseous. "Can't do it." She poured the rest onto the grass.

"A swim would be nice." Sloan pursed her lips. "The pool Aidan and I are building won't be ready for another two weeks, though."

"Hello? Ocean. Two blocks."

"How about our own party?" Sloan's expression brightened. "We've done all we can here. We should all go—"

"Hey, guys." Malina, Carr's FBI agent girlfriend, joined them. "Some shindig."

Malina wore her ever-present gun holster over a white dress shirt paired with tailored black pants. Obviously she'd come directly from work. Her turquoise gaze swept the crowd.

What she searched for, Brenna had no idea, but other than a brief spark of amusement when she spotted Loff, her thoughts weren't apparent.

"You didn't have to come," Sloan said. "We know you're busy."

Malina jerked her shoulders in a shrug. "No problem. Getting rid of this Loff guy is important to all of us. What's the latest?"

"Plenty of people are impressed with Loff at his qualifications," Brenna said. "He's been a treasure hunter a long time and is well-known. Some aren't so thrilled."

"Those are the women he's made a clumsy pass at," Sloan put in.

Malina smiled. "Or the ones who lust after Fortune."

"Ooh." Sloan took hold of Brenna's arm. "We could auction him off on a date. That's great PR."

Brenna frowned in confusion. "Who? Loff?"

Sloan smiled hopefully. "Gavin."

"Hell, no."

Brenna's instinctive, purely jealous reaction brought heat to her cheeks. "This is a serious historical and scientific endeavor. It shouldn't be demeaned with something so pedestrian."

Malina and Sloan exchanged a knowing glance. "Right," they said as one.

Malina patted Brenna's shoulder, clearly sympathetic. She'd been blindsided by her own charming and brilliant guy recently, after all. "I'm headed out to the marina. If we're all here, somebody should be watching the wreck site."

"But Loff and his people are here," Sloan said.

Malina's sharp cop's gaze swept the crowd again. "All of them?"

Suddenly the joyous atmosphere around them stole the air. The tips of Brenna's fingers tingled. Something was off. "Somebody from Loff's camp met with the mayor and got the permit for this party without us knowing."

Sloan stiffened. "What else are they doing behind our backs?"

Malina laid her hand on the butt of her pistol. "Let's find out."

"You guys go," Brenna ordered, already moving away. "I'll get Gavin."

"WE NEED TO GET BACK to the boat," Brenna said, breaking through the crowd around Gavin and grasping his hands.

After hours of talking to locals and the reporter Brenna had suggested, Gavin was past ready to take his anxiety away, to dive into the cool, solitary depths of the sea. He was ready for Brenna's smile and touch. To set aside the argument they'd had, to soothe the frazzled edges of his temper.

But if today had taught him anything, he also recognized he needed to keep his professional goals foremost in his mind.

"Okay," he agreed, drawing her against him. "Folks, this is—"

"Now." Brenna tugged him away. "Sorry," she said as an afterthought to the people gathered. "There's been an equipment malfunction." She worked up a smile. "Only Dr. Fortune can fix it. You understand?"

After they'd darted across the park to Brenna's car, Gavin tucked her into the passenger's seat. She looked too upset to drive. "What's happened?"

"Who's watching the *Heat?*"

Gavin lurched out into traffic. "Watching it?"

"Where are Dennis and Jim?"

"At the storage unit. While everybody was distracted, I figured this was a good time to move everything we've brought up the last few days."

Though a chill remained in her eyes, Brenna nodded. "Good thinking. The pictures and videos Pablo's been working on in order to find Cullen's treasure chest?"

"In the safe in his hotel room. With the *Heat* so visible and Loff popping up every other minute, we decided to keep everything there instead. We also send digital backups to my agent every day."

Abruptly, she leaned over, gripped the back of his head and kissed him hard on the mouth. "You're brilliant."

His pulse jumped, and he had to slam on the brakes to keep from running a red light.

She'd been preoccupied, even distant the last couple of days. Maybe he had, too. His decision to keep bringing up treasure had disenchanted her. All this time he'd been trying to earn her respect, and he'd only succeeded in doing the opposite.

He wasn't sure if he was more aggravated with her or himself.

Sweeping into a parking spot at the marina, he cut the engine, grabbed her hand and they ran. He didn't doubt her instincts for a second.

Something was seriously wrong.

As they rushed across the gangplank onto the *Heat,* he got an eyeful of exactly what.

Chairs and umbrellas were strewn about the deck like a hurricane had tossed everything within its angry wind and was pleased with the chaos that resulted. Windows to the cabin were smashed. Further investigation in the interior revealed kitchen drawers upended on the floor. Refrigerator items, clothes and toiletries thrown all over the bedroom.

Only the sturdy storage lockers on deck where the equipment was kept were unmolested. The vandal had attempted to smash the locks without success.

Fear and fury as he'd never known punched through Gavin's body. His past had brought this to his doorstep, as he had no doubt who was responsible. The knowledge fired his determination to ensure the safety of the treasure he was protecting.

Loff would pay for tainting his goals. For betrayal. For deceit and greed. For insinuating himself into the life Gavin had struggled to make apart from his mentor's.

His furious vision cleared long enough for him to note

Sloan Kendrick pacing the deck as she talked into the cell phone against her ear. Malina Blair, FBI, stood in the center of the chaos. Her expression full of disgust.

Brenna had brought these warriors to him. These defenders of history and truth. Right and wrong.

He had to live up to their expectations now, as well as those of his family and his own.

"The party was a diversion," Brenna said, her voice hushed in shock, jolting him with the ramifications.

"Smoke," Malina added, echoing Pablo's earlier assessment. "Take an inventory, Fortune. See what's missing."

Not trusting himself to speak rationally, Gavin simply nodded.

"We need to call the sheriff," Brenna said.

"What the hell good will *that* do?" Gavin roared. "The legal system hasn't been any help so far."

Brenna blinked those Irish green eyes in shock and hurt.

See, he should have kept his mouth shut.

WITH VENGEANCE DRIVING HIM, the disappointed look in Brenna's eyes haunted Gavin as he spent two days getting the *Heat* back in shape.

It didn't help that he was so angry with himself, with Loff and with the whole damn mess that he was on edge constantly.

The aftermath of their argument—had it even been that?—from Saturday night lingered. He resented her questioning his motives, even as he doubted himself.

Was Brenna right? Was he going too far to stop Loff?

Yet how could he even think that, given Loff's attempted bribery of an entire island and his efforts to steal the treasure Gavin had already uncovered.

Because that certainly was the motive for the boat's vandalism.

Theft, pure and simple. Loff had expected to find and plunder treasure the easy way. The underhanded and illegal way. What else was new?

Not finding what he wanted, the boat had been vandalized.

The fit of temper reminded Gavin of his own as he'd stood on the steps of City Hall beside Brenna and watched Loff's smarminess in action. If he was going to beat his old boss, he had to think clearly, calmly. Coldly.

He had to be more canny, fight dirty.

He said none of this to Brenna, of course. She accepted his assurance that everything was going to work out, helped him repair his boat and continued to share his bed.

Deep inside, though, he burned. Considered. Planned.

And doubted.

Because Loff was driving a wedge between him and his beautiful Irish pixie as surely as the Atlantic ebbed and flowed.

But the last two days had also brought hope. Brenna had held another town meeting, and her fellow islanders had turned up to hear her explain Loff's party had merely been a bribe and that Gavin was the one who'd protect their history.

Pablo was confident his endless hours of watching video gleaned from the ROV at wreck site would pay off. He'd found areas he believed served as storage rooms on *The Carolina* and was betting they'd find Cullen's chest of gold in one of them.

Gavin and Brenna had an appointment at Carr Hamilton's office on Friday to talk about the next legal step they could take and update him on Penelope's genealogical research. Gavin hoped the attorney had good news. Or finding the treasure would be a moot point.

Taking Loff's PR coup seriously, Gavin spent nights at Joe's or the marina bar, getting to know the islanders. He gave phone and satellite interviews. He flirted. He charmed. He did all the things expected of Gavin Fortune.

And hated every minute of it.

His only solace was Brenna—her mind, her body and her spirit.

Last night, though, she'd been asleep when he came to bed. She hadn't turned toward him as she usually did. He'd laid on his back and glared at the ceiling, desperate to find another way to fight this battle with Loff and wishing Gavin Fortune would go to the devil.

Tonight, he decided as he slid open the cabin door, would be different. Tonight, they were settling this business of his supposed obsession with beating Loff. He was the protector, not the aggressor. Saving the treasure was his greatest priority.

The cat greeted him in the main cabin.

Shakes was taking to life at sea—along with a crew who were extremely free with handing out treats—a little too well. Gavin had read somewhere that since cats were natural hunters, owners of overweight pets were encouraged to hide their cat's food, thereby feeding them and getting them to exercise.

Leaning down, he scratched the feline between his scowling yellow eyes. "If you'd take a lap or two around the deck every once in a while, I wouldn't have to resort to desperate measures."

Shakes turned his back and trotted down the hall toward the bedroom.

So maybe the food hiding research had been a little sparse.

Following the cat, Gavin found Brenna in bed, lying on her side and turned away from the empty space where he should be.

Her beautiful hair was pulled into a knot on top of her head. Those probing green eyes closed. He stripped off his shirt, shoes and socks but left on his jeans. Naked conversations with Brenna were inevitably short, and they needed to settle this tension between them.

He slid under the covers and wrapped his arm around her waist from behind, pulling her against his body.

She stiffened before laying her hand over his and linking their fingers. "How was Joe's?"

"Okay." Gently, he kissed the nape of her neck. "Better if you'd been there."

"Gavin Fortune doesn't have a girlfriend."

Propping himself onto his elbow, he rolled her to her back so he could see her face. "Doesn't he?"

Her gaze searched his and whatever she saw had her curling her hand around his neck and pulling him toward her mouth.

Before Gavin could follow through on the invitation, however, there was a pounding at the cabin door. "Hell."

Brenna rolled out of bed and gained her feet. "The vandals?" she whispered tossing a robe over the T-shirt she was wearing.

He didn't see how, though he'd dearly love to kick somebody's ass. Still, concern had him passing Brenna in the hallway and keeping her carefully behind him as they approached the door.

Pablo waved at them from the other side of the glass.

"Is this going to be a habit?" Gavin asked his first mate irritably.

"This time it's good news." Pablo's grin was wide and white beneath the glowing moon. "I think I've found Cullen's treasure."

11

BRENNA WOKE ALONE.

She extended her hand toward the empty pillow next to her and found it cold. But she recalled that Gavin had slept—or at least come to bed—for a while.

After Pablo's appearance, her lover had worked with his friend in the main cabin for hours checking and rechecking Pablo's video research against charts and coordinates, but Gavin had slid into bed late in the night. Despite uncertainty between them, their bodies were like magnets. The irresistible attraction seemed unstoppable. Without a word, they'd turned to each other. She'd breathed his name as they became one, the dreamy weight of him sending her hunger spiraling higher and higher until he'd collapsed on top of her, his breath hot on her skin, his heart hammering in time with her own racing pulse.

They'd solved nothing except temporarily satisfying their libidos. But their need spoke volumes.

She pulled his pillow to her face and inhaled his lingering scent, recalling the pleasure of his hands, the heat of his body.

How much longer?

How little time she did have before memories and traces of him were all she had left?

Not much. Not long.

Expecting he'd already left on his mission, she was surprised to hear low voices as she crawled out of bed. More than Gavin and Pablo. The whole team, probably. She moved blindly to the shower, not wanting to face the truth she knew lay beyond the bedroom door.

They were going after the treasure.

Pablo had been diligently reviewing the videos and pictures they'd taken over the last few weeks, and after various observations, scientific calculations, he'd found a darkened area that matched the estimations of Cullen's chest of gems and gold.

Not so long ago, Brenna would have been exhilarated by this news.

Today, she was depressed.

When a tired, worried stranger with her exact features stared back at her from the mirror, she made a concerted effort to mask her troubles with makeup and eyedrops.

She found an aqua-blue sundress hanging in the closet and put it on. The color was bright. Maybe she wouldn't look as worried on the outside as she was on the inside.

It was all coming to a head. Like a hurricane, swallowing up everything in its destructive path.

Bearing down on her fears, she opened the bedroom door and walked down the hall. Midsentence, Gavin stopped and stared at her.

He already wore a wet suit, the top half hanging around his waist, leaving his impressive chest bare.

Even through the tension, she wanted him. Part of her wished she didn't, and that she could go back to her easy, mundane life. But the very air around her was heavy with his presence.

Would his name always be on her lips?

"So…" she began, forcing cheer into her tone as she walked toward the group. "Big treasure dive, huh?"

"We'll bring you back an emerald to match your eyes,' Pablo said, waggling his eyebrows.

Dennis nudged Pablo, and Jim looked out the window.

The silence lengthened. More than anything, Brenna wanted to lose herself in Gavin's arms, to pull him back into bed, where their agreement was assured. But they continued to stare, frozen, at each other.

"We should get going," Dennis said, tucking a laptop beneath his arm.

Jim and Pablo followed quickly.

"I'm right behind you," Gavin said as the guys headed out. He turned to Brenna, closed the distance between them and tugged her against his bare chest. "Come with me."

She wasn't exactly thrilled *he* was going. How could she be there to support him? "I should stay here. Somebody should be watching the boat."

"We'll call Dwayne."

"He needs supervision."

"So Finn." When she remained silent, Gavin added, "I'd really like you to be with me."

"I don't want *you* to go."

He sighed and leaned back. "Wouldn't you have liked to be there when your grandmother's broach was brought up?"

Her stomach clenched. "That's not even remotely fair."

"You get corn dogs and cotton candy at the fair. This is war."

And love?

Oh, no. She wasn't going there. Not now.

The apprehension in his body, in his face, undid her. "If you get arrested, I'm only there to get a tan."

"Naturally."

"I'm not defending you in federal court."

"I wouldn't expect you to."

"Fine. I'll throw on a suit."

She flounced—yes, no other word for it—into the bedroom. Stripping off her sundress and underwear, she put on her favorite silver lamé bikini—if the Feds did show up to arrest them, she wanted to look good in her mug shot.

After she pulled the sundress back on, she returned to the main cabin.

Gavin embraced her, lowering his face to hers. His taste stirred her hunger, though she knew the breach between them was wide.

Desperation crawled up her throat. She swallowed it and held tight to him instead.

Panic would get them nowhere.

As they parted, he smoothed his hand down her hair, then tugged the ends lightly. "Smile."

She made an effort, though it wasn't her best. Gavin tried not to look disappointed, and she pretended not to notice.

He linked their hands as they walked outside. Pablo, bless him, kept up a running commentary as they lugged their diving gear to Al's boat. The harbormaster had agreed to take the team out to the wreck site without any questions.

Which was wise, considering he could honestly tell any number of lawyers and/or judges that he had no prior knowledge he was aiding and abetting a once-respected Miami research team by defying a court order and stealing a pirate's treasure because they were concerned an unethical colleague might get there first.

Not even über-successful, formerly morally ambiguous litigator Carr Hamilton could hope to get them out of this one.

As Al backed the boat out of his slip, Gavin squeezed Brenna's hand. She apparently didn't have to say anything for him to realize the apprehensive direction of her thoughts. That connection, that sense of knowing each other as no one else did, was only one of many reasons she stood on the precipice of falling in love.

If she lost her balance, she was going down.

"Hey," he said in her ear. When she looked up at him, he

brought their joined hands to his lips. "You know I'm going to make this right, don't you?"

The golden truth shone from in his eyes so intently, she blinked.

A swooping sensation, much like one she'd felt on a roller coaster—or perhaps if she'd dived off a cliff—rolled through her stomach.

Well, damn.

She managed a nod, even as the staved-off panic zipped through her heart.

He grinned. "You've got Gavin Fortune in charge, remember."

Despite the seriousness of the moment, the dread, the hope and the wonder all rolled into one, she found the presence of mind to roll her eyes. "And if this were a bikini competition or America's Next Nude Surfer contest, he'd be perfect. Right now, however, I'd prefer if the brilliant and smart-beyond-his-years Gavin Randall made an appearance."

Wisely, he didn't point out she was breaking her own third-person rule.

"Yes, ma'am," he said, then kissed her cheek.

With her heart committed, the rest of her fell in line.

She allowed herself to feel the anticipation of the hunt. What if they found the chest? What if, after all these years of mystery and speculation, she was part of the team that recovered Captain Cullen's famed treasure?

Of course, she'd never be able to tell anyone without risking prosecution....

She shoved the consequences aside. The fact that she'd dozens of times advised her students to do the exact opposite wasn't lost on her.

Al anchored the boat a few yards from the wreck site, and Gavin encouraged her to head to the deck and make a production out of fluffing her towel, arranging her book, bottle of water and sunscreen while they hoisted on their scuba tanks and slipped over the side.

Standing in the center of her towel, she lifted her arms over her head and yawned, as if her biggest decision the whole day would be whether to lie on her back or her stomach. Of course, anybody who knew perpetually cranky Al would know that his interest in taking a woman on a sunbathing pleasure cruise ranked right up there with launching himself to Mars via a bungee cord.

But maybe nobody would look too closely at the—

A warm hand pressing at the small of her back made her jump. "For heaven's sake, Gavin," she said when she recognized it was him. "What are you—"

"An award-winning performance isn't necessary," he said, wrapping her towel around her shoulders.

"Excuse me?"

"The sunbathing. You failed to mention your bikini contains less fabric than a dinner napkin. I can't keep my crew focused like this."

Score one for silver lamé. She drew her hand up his wet suit. "What about you? Can you concentrate?"

He sucked in a quick breath. "Brenna, please."

She brushed her lips across his jaw. "I shouldn't be the only one who's a wreck."

"Ha, ha."

Stepping back, she shrugged off the towel. His gaze followed the move. She laid one hand on her hip. The other she used to trail her fingers down her thigh. His pupils dilated.

It seemed muscle tone wasn't only an advantage in tumbling.

"I'm waving at every boat that passes by," she said, arranging herself on her towel. "While I'm worrying up here, you can worry down there."

"That's not fair."

She peeked at him over the top of her sunglasses. "Then maybe you should hunt down a corn dog and some cotton candy to console yourself."

HOURS WENT BY.

How long could they stay down there?

Brenna couldn't imagine those little tanks holding that much air.

Screw the performance, she thought as she paced, while Al lay peacefully in the sun reading a fishing magazine. "We've got to do something."

"Like what?"

"Go down there."

"With what?" Al asked, reclining in a deck chair. "They've got all the scuba tanks."

"We can swim along the surface. I just want to see."

"There's sharks in that water." Without shifting his gaze from the magazine, Al pointed over the side of the boat. "I'm not gettin' in."

Sharks?

She was worried about the Coast Guard, the Feds, the island cops and Loff. Deadly marine life hadn't even crossed her mind.

Until now.

"I thought you navigated around here all the time," she protested. "Surely you're not scared."

"I navigate in a *boat,*" Al said, finally glancing over long enough to glare at her. "Swimmers, surfers and divers are idiots."

The vision of Gavin and the team being confronted by the blunt nose and dead eyes of a massive great white made her stomach roll. Why had she let them go? Crazy men, chasing historical tidbits. Buttons and broaches, a possible chest of gold coins. Which, let's face it, couldn't still be intact. The coins and jewels were probably scattered along the ocean floor. Unless Cullen had sealed his ill-gotten gains in a solid metal box or—

Hang on, there weren't great white sharks in these waters.

Just black tips, hammerheads, maybe a thresher or two. Or ten.

Al went back to reading, and Brenna paced, trying to block out images of failing air tanks, sharks, evil electric eels that did the bidding of a purple underwater octopus queen.

No, maybe that was a movie cartoon she'd seen.

Still, they should have sent down the ROV. It's maneuverability was nearly as good as human hands. No oxygen tank required. Plus, it didn't bleed, so too bad for the sharks. Come to think of it, why hadn't they done that?

Oh, right. Because they were being covert.

And illegal.

Hearing a splash at the boat's stern, Brenna rushed in that direction. Before peeking over the side, she closed her eyes, wishing she'd at least had the presence of mind to ask for a blessing from Sister Mary Katherine before the journey.

A cold, wet blast of water hit the center of her chest, and her eyes flew open.

Gavin bobbed in the water. His grin was as wide as Texas. He drew his arm back and tossed something at her, which she caught.

From the weight and size, she knew it was a coin. Her heart pounded as she studied its mucky, grayish-green surface. With her thumbnail, she scraped off the grime.

Gold flashed in the afternoon sun.

Her gaze flew to Gavin. Certain she would see the same glint in his eyes, she smiled. "You found it. The treasure."

12

THE CHAMPAGNE FLOWED late into the night.

Brenna buried her concerns and provided both food and drink to the maritime warriors.

To the single gold coin Gavin had tossed her, handfuls had been added. The guys had spent most of the day and well on toward sunset pulling up treasure, which had, just as Pablo suspected, been originally stowed in a hiding place deep beneath the bow of *The Carolina*.

The ROV had been retrieved and used to excavate many of the coins, as well as a variety of jewelry. A diamond-and-emerald necklace whose individual gems were easily the size of Brenna's thumbnail had been welcomed with awe.

And there was more.

It would likely take several days to recover it all, and how long they could keep the find under wraps was a point of order that only Brenna seemed to be worried about.

A few weeks ago, she would have sacrificed anything to protect the ship. But she didn't like the slippery slope they found themselves on, one that seemed to get steeper every day. Shouldn't they be watching Loff to be sure he didn't make off with the treasure and leaving further discoveries until the courts could decide the ship's ownership? Weren't they stealing? Was beating Loff worth prison?

After an exhilarating day of diving and discovery, the team, including Al, were passed out on the cabin floor aboard the *Miami Heat*. Brenna slipped pillows under everyone's heads and laid blankets over their bodies.

Tomorrow would bring more work. And probably champagne-induced headaches.

But no way, despite possible retribution and complications, could she deny them this moment of triumph.

She knelt next to Gavin, who was sprawled on his back near the sofa. "You want to come to bed?" she whispered in his ear.

He grunted.

She should leave him be.

But as she started to lean back, she reconsidered.

The discovery of the treasure meant triumph for him, and the end for them. She wanted every moment to count. She wanted his warmth and arms around her. Loving him was complicated, certainly full of heartache, but she had him now.

Well, very shortly she would. If she played her cards right.

As Pablo snored on the couch above them, she pressed her lips gently to Gavin's.

"Brenna," he mumbled in his sleep.

With a smile, she drew her mouth along his jawline. "I'm here. Come with me. I need you."

He reached for her, burying his hand in her hair. "I was dreaming about you."

"You don't have to."

"You were a mermaid," he continued, and she swallowed a laugh at his sleepy tone. "I was about to set sail, and you were calling me to shore."

"Was I?"

"Gavin Fortune wants me to go away. He needs me. But you want me to stay."

Brenna bit her tongue to keep from asking anything else.

She wasn't sure she could face having him admit she mattered to him, here in this unguarded state, only to take it back when the next adventure called.

"I need you now," she said, then she flicked her tongue against his earlobe.

His eyes flew open. He blinked, confused, then desire brightened his eyes. "Brenna."

She helped him gain his feet. "Come to bed."

Taking his hand, she led him down the hall. She expected him to collapse on the bed and drift back to his dreams, but he shoved the door closed with his foot, then jerked her back against him. His body was hard and hot, and she bit back a moan as his hands slid over her hips and thighs.

He moved her hair aside and skimmed his mouth along her shoulder. "I found the treasure."

She fought for breath. "I know. I was there."

"Not that one." He spun her, backing her to the bed. "This one."

Looming over her, he pressed her into the mattress. Desire punched through her body. What did they have, really, but this? This sensual assault. A carnal need.

Yet she knew there was more.

For her, anyway.

Though the barriers between them seemed unsurpassable, she wrapped her legs around his waist, bumping her hips against his. A spasm of desire shot down her spine.

She was wearing only a long T-shirt, so he easily lifted it over her head and tossed it aside. She unzipped his jeans, and he shoved them and his shirt to the floor.

Skin to skin, they rolled to their sides.

He clutched her against his chest. "Even diving for priceless treasure, all I could think about was you in that silver bikini."

"No kidding?" She pressed her lips to the base of his throat, where his pulse beat hard and strong. "All I could think about were sharks."

"We take a speargun with us."

The image of him jabbing a big stick, probably ineffectually, into the body of a teeth-laden shark momentarily distracted her from his roaming hands.

At least until he drew his fingers between her legs.

The stimulation sent her desire soaring. Her breath caught. Her body tightened.

Wanting and desperate, she rolled on top of him. After making use of a condom from the bedside table, she lifted her hips and plunged down. Nothing could ever be so fulfilling. No other man could possibly cause the same burst of pleasure and need.

He linked their hands, which he drew above his head as she rocked against him. His golden gaze stayed locked with hers. The intensity of the moment overwhelmed her mind, body and soul.

When their climaxes met, pushing them up and over, she let the pulses roll through her. Relentless like the ocean waves. Formidable and predictable as the tides.

She would always want him, always feel the urge to call him to her.

Like the mermaid to the sailor. The sea to the sand.

A battle and triumph that would never be fully reconciled, but one that could coexist. If only the pull was strong enough.

IN THE MORNING, Gavin sent his hardworking crew out with coffee and stale doughnuts.

He felt guilty, but couldn't dwell.

His job, his reputation, everything he'd fought for in his life was at stake, and *now* his romantic heart was asserting itself, challenging his goals. Beautiful and determined Brenna couldn't have shown up in high school, when he'd felt inferior, out of place and directionless.

No, she'd picked the height of the Gavin Fortune nonsense and triumph to appear and change his life.

She challenged truths he'd already proved. She stimulated his brain and his body. She made him whole and made him question…well, *all* his priorities.

As he sat on the sofa, cupping a warm mug of coffee in his hand, she appeared in the cabin, dressed in shorts and a sparkling turquoise tank top.

"Where'd everybody go?" she asked.

"To do their jobs. Coffee's hot," he added with a nod toward the kitchen counter.

"You wanted to talk to me in private?" she asked as she turned with her own mug of coffee in her hand.

"Yes." His brain was a little fuzzy from the diving and champagne of the day before, but the confrontation brewing between them all week couldn't wait another minute. "How could you ask me whether winning or protecting treasure was more important?"

"Because I wonder if it is."

His jaw clenched. "You don't trust me. Or believe me. If we don't have that, what do we have?"

"What we always had—a temporary, hot and powerful hookup."

So everything. And nothing.

To hear her be so blasé, so matter-of-fact, so honest annoyed the hell out of him. "Don't you want more?" he asked her.

"Does it matter?" She fired the question back, the green in her eyes bright and fierce. "There is no more with you."

"And I'm sorry, but I have to do this."

He wasn't angry at her, he knew. He was mad at himself. He'd been honest, too. Truthful and careful not to make promises. Was that the kind of relationship worthy of a woman like Brenna?

With a sigh of resignation that broke his heart, she sat next to him on the sofa. "I get it. You have a mission. Nothing can or will measure up to that."

Instead of being purposeful, that sounded pathetic. Yet

the life he'd led over the last several years had been amazing. Exciting, ever-changing and full of accomplishment. Why did holding Brenna make him feel so whole and so lousy at the same time? "We don't even agree on the way to get the treasure."

"No, we don't." She rose and moved away to look out the windows. "But I don't get a vote. This is your project. I am, and always was, only here to observe and make sure the men of *The Carolina* are treated with dignity and respect. On that score, I have no doubt you'll do the right thing. Frankly, I don't care about the treasure."

"You'd rather me leave it down there, for vultures like Loff to scoop up?"

She studied him over her shoulder. "You need the money?"

"Well...no. Of course not."

"Your clients need the money?"

"I don't know. It's still theirs."

Her lips turned up in a sad smile. "Is it really?"

He jolted to his feet. "Leave the treasure down there. That's what you're suggesting?" He hunted treasure. That's what he did. Who he was. "What good will that do? Captain Cullen's life's work, by the way. You're Miss Self-Righteous Historical Society Queen. Who, exactly, would it benefit to leave all that gold on the bottom on the ocean floor?"

"You."

What the hell?

She set aside her mug and closed the distance between them. "Listen to yourself, Gavin. You don't need the money. You don't care about wealth because you already have it. Maybe there's honor in completing this contract, but your success won't be diminished if the treasure isn't recovered. You want to beat Loff. That's what you need. That's what this whole thing is about."

"You want to beat him, too."

"Sure. But I've lived with his betrayal all my life. I know

what kind of man he is, and I know that even if I succeed here, it's likely he'll go on to another town, hurt another family. But you think you can stop him. And if not him, whoever comes along after him. If you're smart enough, fast enough, clever enough, well-funded enough, you'll get them all. And nobody else can do it just the way you would. That's why you're so committed to your hunts." She gripped his hand. "It's admirable, really. Arrogant, but admirable."

His heart pounding inordinately hard, he jerked his hand away. "I don't think I like you very much right now."

She pressed her lips to his cheek. "That's because I'm right. Teacher's prerogative." Grabbing her cup, she poured her remaining coffee into an insulated travel mug, then headed to the door. "I have some errands to run. I'll see you at Carr's office about the legal issues. The appointment's at two."

"What time are you coming back to get me?"

She fluttered her lashes and smiled sweetly. "I'm not."

"But I don't have a way to get there."

"Then you probably should have told me you liked me very much."

GAVIN RAN TO THE LAWYER'S office.

When he showed up sweaty and out of breath, Brenna would feel guilty for stranding him. Plus, the workout burned off his anger.

Mostly, anyway.

Of course he wasn't the *only* one who could make sure the historical treasures of the past made it into the right hands. But he was the most motivated and had the best equipment.

Besides, he took pride in his work. Uncovering secrets of the past gave him a rush and made him feel as if he might someday actually live up to his family legacy. He liked his life, thank you very much, and just because Brenna had slammed him between the eyes with her passion and determination was no reason to question everything he'd accomplished over the last decade.

So why was he nearly certain that one day soon he'd have to choose between his job and his lover?

A temporary hot and powerful hook-up, she'd said.

He refused to believe things between them were that simple. Or that doomed. He'd never felt so connected to a woman before. At first, they were conquests, then they were fun, then they were…just there.

To compare Brenna to the casual relationships in his past was an insult. To him and her.

Still the specter of his imminent choice lingered over him like a cloud. Like the ghosts from *The Carolina.*

As he arrived in the sand-and-shell-strewn parking lot that housed Carr Hamilton's office, Gavin braced his hands on his knees to catch his breath. Hell, it was hot.

He was actually looking forward to rainy London after this project.

Already moving on, are we? his conscience taunted. *Scared, maybe? I wonder if what's right in front of you is way more precious than gold or gems or any historical knickknack you think you need to find?*

Light-headed, that's what he was. Diving in the morning, running in the afternoon. Probably not a good idea. He wasn't twenty anymore.

Wiping stinging sweat from the corner of his eye, he trudged up the steps to the quad-plex, which housed not only the attorney's office but Brenna's dad's real estate office, as well. A family counselor and a…a For Rent sign completed the group.

Gavin stared hard at the rental sign.

He recalled Penelope telling him an insurance agent had run his business from there—at least until he'd been caught in a diamond smuggling and art theft conspiracy this past spring.

As small as Palmer's Island was, life here never seemed to be boring.

Shaking aside the curiosity to see the now-empty office,

he headed inside, then turned toward Carr's door on the left. The attorney, his secretary—whom Gavin had met the night of the town hall meeting—and Brenna stood in the elegant waiting room.

Surrounded by a gold and jewel-toned ambience that could easily translate to any big-city, high-dollar office in the world, the trio were dressed for a business meeting. Carr wore one of his seemingly perpetual dark and tailored designer suits. The secretary looked trim and professional in a navy jacket and skirt, and even Brenna had changed since this morning, into a charcoal-gray wrap dress and high heeled pumps that extended the length of her already fantastic legs.

Though he was exhausted, frustrated and worried, his body didn't care about his mental state as he went hard.

Brenna, by contrast, planted her hands on her hips as she turned. Her shocked gaze raked him from head to toe, lingering on his casual-in-the-extreme shorts and tank top. "You *jogged* here?"

"Yeah."

"Why didn't you get Pablo to bring you?"

"He drove into Charleston to inventory the artifacts at the storage unit."

She stared at Gavin in disbelief. "And he couldn't drop you off on the way?"

In hindsight, as sweat rolled down his face, threatening to drip onto Carr's plush carpet, his plan to make her feel guilty seemed silly at best. "It's barely two miles from the marina to here," he found himself saying as Carr's secretary handed him a towel.

"I'm sure I can find a water bottle," Carr said, moving toward his office, after a sympathetic wince in Gavin's direction. "I'll give you guys a few minutes to…clear this up."

His secretary followed as if the tails of her boss's suit were on fire.

Gavin was faced with the fiery green of Brenna's eyes.

Weakly, he cleared his throat. "Don't you feel guilty for not picking me up at the marina?"

He watched her pupils dilate as she stared at him.

Hang on. He knew that look. *That* was desire, not anger.

Belying the heat in her eyes, she poked her finger in the center of his chest. "If only I had your mother's phone number."

"What for?"

"To text her a picture of this." Her hand swept his body. "She'd disown you."

He grabbed Brenna's hand and pulled her close, though not close enough to touch. "You've seen me sweaty before."

Her breath caught.

Oh, yeah. She was seriously aroused.

She shoved him back.

And seriously angry.

"Just because I think you're insanely hot doesn't mean everybody else will," she whispered heatedly after a quick glance at Carr's partially open office door. "Look at the furniture in this place. It's probably worth more than your boat."

He cast her a smug glance. "Insanely hot, huh?"

"Don't sit on anything," she warned as she headed toward the office.

"I'll replace anything I ruin."

"Have I told you lately that you having more money than a king is annoying?"

"You've never told me that."

"Then consider yourself informed." As she crossed the threshold into the attorney's office—which had an old-school, mahogany-and-gold, heavy furniture look Gavin's grandfather would have admired—Brenna's demeanor flicked like a switch. "Thank you both so much for seeing us today. I know you're busy."

The secretary left them alone, closing the office door behind her.

"I always have time for you, Brenna," Carr said, holding her hands and brushing his lips across her cheek.

Though he knew Carr was in a fully committed relationship with his live-in girlfriend, Gavin still felt a spark of annoyance.

The lawyer met his gaze over Brenna's head. "Working hard, are you, Dr. Fortune?"

"Always."

"Doing what, exactly?" Seemingly casual, Carr moved behind his desk, extending his hand for Gavin and Brenna to take seats in front. "You're currently bound by a court order that prevents you from exploring *The Carolina*."

While Brenna sat, Gavin chose to stand. "I was running."

"And this morning you were fishing?" Carr raised his eyebrows at Gavin's scowl. "It's a small island."

Gavin nodded. He'd faced down lawyers, and even actual sharks, many times before. "So small you're interested in my leisure time?"

"Me?" Carr displayed mock surprise. "No, I couldn't care less. Law enforcement, however, might take a different view." His eyes narrowed. "They're not stupid. My girlfriend is an FBI agent, and they've already been notified by the attorney general to look out for maritime activity in the area. So…" He paused as he leaned back in his chair. "If your team is tempted to continue exploring the wreckage, I'd advise you to take care. Two federal judges are now fighting over their rulings, so this is going to get some serious attention by higher courts. Either one or both of them could toss you and your crew in jail, impound your boat, your equipment—right down to your computers and flippers—and let you cool your heels until next winter before anything's decided."

Gavin cast a hard glance at Brenna. How much had she told her friend?

"Nothing," she said, clearly reading his mind. "Carr is simply warning us about the ramifications of our legal position."

"*My* legal position," Gavin corrected. "You know how important your help and support is to me, but I won't let you risk your reputation." He looked over the desk at Carr. "Maybe we shouldn't have involved the judge."

"Loff started the process," the lawyer said. "You had no choice but to respond. What you do in the aftermath, however, could affect your life and your business for years to come."

"I know what I'm doing."

"Fine." Carr directed his attention back to Brenna. "Besides the work with the court orders, my staff and I are trying to discover the whereabouts of the documents Loff submitted to the court in Chicago."

"Doesn't anybody think these conveniently missing documents make Loff's whole claim suspicious?" Brenna asked.

Carr nodded. "Certainly. Proving fraud is an entirely different matter. Which is why I'm flying to Chicago this evening."

As Gavin's gaze moved to the lawyer again, Brenna leaned forward. "You don't have to. We appreciate your help, but—"

"This is my island, too," Carr said. "My history."

"But surely somebody will see how ridiculous Loff's claim is," Brenna protested.

"Who?" Carr asked with raised eyebrows. "And when? No one's going to question a federal judge's ruling. The only reason I'm even getting a meeting with a clerk up there is because one of the prosecutors and I went to law school together." Carr's gaze shifted from her to Gavin. "I'm going to do all I can, but I think you both should be prepared for a long, possibly fruitless battle."

Gavin had known the moment Loff showed up that he'd cause nothing but trouble. Gavin just hadn't realized how much. "Clearly I should have gone to law school instead of wasting my time with all that chemistry and physics."

Carr's smile was sardonic. "Why bother when you can hire or charm who you need?"

Okay, so he and his attorney—wait, the *island* attorney—weren't destined to get along. That was fine, he guessed, but he couldn't be happy that one of Brenna's friends resented him. The rest of her friends didn't have a problem with him. What was Hamilton's deal?

"Don't give him a hard time," Brenna said absently to Carr. Then she huffed out an annoyed breath. "Why was Loff able to get a ruling in Chicago, anyway?"

"Because that's the corporate headquarters of the Sea Oats Shipping Company," Gavin said.

"Exactly." Carr looked a bit surprised—by Brenna's defense of Gavin or the fact that he understood at least some aspect of business and law, he wasn't sure. "As far as the plan to watch and harass Loff, his boat is due to arrive in the marina tomorrow. The fire department will be waiting for it."

"How do you know that?" Brenna asked.

Carr shrugged. "He had to reserve a slip with Al."

"I love this island," Brenna said with a smile.

"Don't we all?" Again, Carr's hard gaze slid briefly to Gavin. "The fire department will be performing a thorough inspection on Loff's boat, whose arrival seems to indicate he's through *fishing* and throwing parties and instead intending to pursue the treasure."

What treasure? Gavin thought but made sure to focus on Hamilton's information.

"But they also have to look over everything in the marina, so you might want to make sure your fire prevention equipment is up-to-date."

Gavin nodded. "It is."

"One final item—the Sisters are holding a prayer vigil," Carr said.

"Whose sisters?" Gavin asked.

"The nuns," Brenna clarified. "Prayer is sort of their go-to strategy."

Again, Gavin nodded. "Ah."

"You have a lot to learn about island life." Carr leaned back in his chair. "Too bad you won't be around long enough to put this growing knowledge to good use."

"YOUR BUDDY CARR DOESN'T like me very much."

With Gavin beside her, Brenna pulled her car out onto Beach Road. "No, he doesn't. He knows you're violating the court order. He's worried about sticking his neck out for you and the historical society." *He's worried about me.*

"He doesn't like that we're together."

"No, he doesn't."

"Your other friends aren't against me. Why him?"

'Cause I didn't break down and tell them I'm in love with you. "Don't worry about it."

Gavin laid his arm on the back of her seat. "Why him?"

"He's in a great relationship. He wants everybody else to be, too."

She felt, more than saw, Gavin grow still.

And we're not.

She didn't like his obsession with the treasure. She didn't like his compulsion to beat Loff to the point of sacrificing everything. Especially her.

But they were bound by *The Carolina,* their duty and promise to protect the wreck, its lost crewmen and even its treasure. No matter her personal heartache, she could at least hang on to that.

"Let's focus on Loff's boat coming in," she said. "The inspection might slow him down for a few hours, a day at the most, but he's certain to head out to the wreck site soon."

"We'll keep a round-the-clock watch," Gavin said, and she was relieved he was letting the subject of their relationship drop. "Can we count on the sheriff's department?"

"I'll call Tyler when we get to the boat, but I'm sure he's still willing to help."

"And in the meantime, we hope Carr comes up with something in Chicago."

"If anybody can make something happen on the legal front, it's Carr."

"We don't have a great relationship?" Gavin asked abruptly as she pulled into the marina parking lot.

Did he really expect her to answer that question positively? Did she?

A hot hookup had been fine, but once she realized her heart wanted more, and he wasn't willing to give her what she needed, wasn't she betraying herself?

She shut off the engine and turned to him. Could she really see him, be around him, and not *be* with him?

She was about to find out.

"No, we don't have a great relationship."

He slid his thumb across her cheek. "Why not?"

"You need to find treasure. I need...something else."

"I need you."

"But not enough."

He bowed his head. "I don't want to hurt you."

Too late.

"I have to do this," he added. His voice was seeped in regret, and she felt an answering pang in her own heart. "I have obligations. To my team, my family and myself." When he stared at her his eyes were glowing with a swirling mix of green and gold. "Why can't we just—

She shook her head. "I'm through selling myself short for a guy."

"So that's it?" he returned, his tone now hard. "It's over?"

"Yes. You'll be gone in a few days, and—"

"You heard Carr. This could drag out a long time. Years, even."

"Which is why you're going to help your team recover the rest of Cullen's treasure, then move on to Lord Whoever's missing jewelry. Eventually, Pablo will lock up everything in storage and sail back to Miami."

"It's the *Star of Ariana* for Lord Westmore. And how did you know I was thinking of leaving soon?"

"Because this could take years. The lawyers will battle, and the courts will decide. And where's the adventure in that?" She smiled sadly. "I know you. I'm going back to my house tonight. I'll continue helping with *The Carolina,* but I can't—" She swallowed the lump in her throat. "We can't be together anymore."

13

"YOU'RE THE ONLY GIRL I want to be with."

Penelope shifted her gaze from her and Finn's joined hands to his handsome face. Her heart throbbed.

"You know that, don't you?" he added.

"Yes."

His thumb slid back and forth across the back of her hand. "You're my girlfriend, right?"

Would she ever get used to that word in conjunction with her? And him? Them. She had a *them*.

With extreme effort, she managed to suppress the heat crawling up her neck. "Right."

They were sitting in their favorite spot at the marina—at the end of the dock, legs swinging off the edge. The sun was beginning to sink in the distance, and a blessed breeze had finally kicked up off the water. Finn had gotten off duty a bit earlier, and though she'd continued her research into Loff's family history until he'd shown up, her heart hadn't been in the work.

Brenna and Shakespeare Fuzzyboots' departure from Dr. Fortune's boat had been quite a distraction.

"So, I want us to have a real commitment," Finn said.

"We do."

She laid her head on his shoulder. Seeing Brenna's sadness

made Penelope all the more grateful for her own happiness. She longed to dispel the pall cast over the marina by her friend's absence.

Wrapping his arm around her waist, Finn pulled her close. "Your acceptance of me, and my crappy past, means everything to me."

"We've been through this. I care about the man you are today. Plus, the commitment it took for the journey. Crook to cop. Pretty impressive."

"Yeah, well, speaking of commitment—"

"Excuse me? Deputy Hastings?"

Penelope and Finn turned to see Tammy, one of the waitresses from Coconut Joe's, standing behind them. Finn rose, then helped Penelope to her feet. "Yes, ma'am. Can I help you?"

"Maybe I can help you." She gave Finn a flirtatious smile, which dimmed after a glare from Penelope. "Man, all the cute ones are taken. Anyway, it's about that guy—Dan Loff."

"What about him?" Finn asked casually, though Penelope heard an edge to his voice.

"He came in the restaurant earlier with a group of people and I waited on them. They were all pretty picky and kinda snooty—you know, can I have my chicken grilled without oil or butter, then they complained when it was dry." She rolled her eyes. "So, when the check comes, this Loff guy is all showy about pulling out his platinum credit card."

"Sounds just like him," Penelope muttered.

"Yeah, he's kind of a jerk. Which is why I was happy to tell him the card had been rejected."

Finn angled his head. "No kidding."

"Some guy that was with him paid, but I thought it was strange, ya know?"

"I know," Finn agreed.

"Plus this Loff guy tried to make a scene about it—something's wrong with our credit card machine, or maybe I don't know how to work it." Tammy's dark eyes flashed with annoyance. "Ticked me off in a big way."

"He has that effect," Penelope said. "Did Joe get involved?"

"Nah." Tammy waved her hand. "Loff's friend, whose credit card did work, calmed him down, so it wasn't anything. But still…"

Finn and Penelope exchanged a glance. "Still," he said.

"We really appreciate you coming down here to tell us," Penelope said. She had no idea what Loff's lack of credit meant, but the detail was something to note. *Hadn't he just spent thousands on a party for the whole island?*

Tammy shrugged. "Well, Sister's orders and all. And Dr. Fortune's much nicer. Do you know if he's around?"

Finn shook his head doubtfully. "I think he went into Charleston."

Penelope smiled despite her shock. Last time she'd seen their fearless leader, he was flopped in a lounge chair with a bottle of beer and glaring at the sea. But she supposed the last thing they needed was one of Dr. Fortune's fans poking around. Or attempting to console him over his breakup with Brenna. "We'll tell him you stopped by."

"Okay, thanks." After a final wave, Tammy turned and walked down the pier.

"What do you make of that?" Finn asked Penelope when the waitress was out of earshot.

"I'm not sure. Probably nothing."

"Probably."

But by the look on Finn's face, he seemed to doubt his words as much as she did hers. Could this be the advantage they needed to gain over Loff?

Finn linked their hands. "We should probably tell Pablo right away."

Penelope glanced at him. "Not Dr. Fortune?"

"I think he's going to be incapacitated tonight."

"She loves him," Penelope said with a sigh. "It's such a shame they can't be together."

"Sure they can—if they want to badly enough. How do you know she loves him?"

Penelope focused on his face, the icy blue eyes that watched her so intently.

And she knew.

"Because I recognize the signs. I love you."

He smiled. "That's good to hear, because I love you, too, and I want you to marry me."

THE DAYS AFTER LEAVING Gavin dragged by for Brenna. She helped the crew of the *Heat* whenever she could, and avoided him at all costs. Even Shakes missed him.

Of course, he could just be longing for ahi tuna.

Carr provided updates from Chicago, but he'd so far had no luck in locating the missing papers Loff had used to make his ownership claim. Why nobody had thought to make copies at the time of the court ruling was suspiciously neglectful.

Loff's boat had shown up in the marina. Al, Thad and others had caught him heading to the wreck site three times already. Loff was livid, complaining to Gavin, the sheriff and even the mayor. While the elected officials promised—somehow with straight faces—to look into the matter, Gavin, so Brenna had heard, simply stared him down until he ceased his rant and slunk away.

Why Loff never thought to turn around and spy on Gavin's team in retaliation was anybody's guess.

Brenna pushed through whatever busywork she could manage, including some summer tutoring, tossed and turned during the night and waited for the morning she'd show up at the marina and find Gavin, his team and his boat gone.

By the time Sloan called on Friday and invited her to lunch, Brenna was on the verge of untying the *Heat* from the dock herself, simply to end the anticipation of misery.

Arriving at Mabel's Diner, she found not only Sloan, but

Andrea, Penelope and even Malina sitting in the large corner booth. Absolutely not in the mood to chat with a bunch of people, Brenna nearly turned around and left. But, as if on cue, the women spotted her and waved.

Something was up.

And Brenna was positive it wouldn't be her mood.

"This is quite a gathering," she said with forced cheer as she slid into the booth beside Andrea.

Sloan and Malina exchanged a brief look, then Sloan shrugged. "It's an intervention."

"Bye." Brenna started to rise, but Malina ordered her to sit, so she did. None of the rest of them were willing—probably— to keep her here by force. Carr's gun-toting FBI girlfriend she wasn't so sure about, however.

"Have some sweet tea," Andrea suggested, pushing a filled plastic cup toward her.

Brenna stared miserably into the amber liquid. "Is this spiked with anything?"

Andrea patted her hand. "No, but Mabel's got whiskey standing by if necessary."

"She doesn't have a liquor license," Brenna pointed out.

"This is an emergency," Sloan said.

"Fine." Brenna took a sip, refusing to admit she already felt better with the sugary drink in front of her and her friends surrounding her. "How 'bout those Cougars?"

"As in cats?" Malina asked, narrowing her eyes in confusion.

"She means the College of Charleston mascot," Penelope explained. "It's a traditional conversation opener in the South to talk about sports."

"It's summer," Sloan said. "Are the Cougars even playing anything right now?

"We need to stay on topic," Andrea said.

"I agree," Penelope interjected.

Malina frowned. "I didn't go off on a tangent. Brenna did."

"No doubt on purpose." Andrea laid her hand over Brenna's and this time held on. "She's going through a difficult time."

With embarrassing tears forming behind her eyes, Brenna stared at the table. Janey, their waitress, arrived to take orders. Normally, she would have stayed to chat and exchange island gossip, but apparently she'd heard Brenna's news along with everybody else.

"Gavin Fortune," Sloan said the moment Janey had moved off.

Silence descended over the table.

After a bracing sip of tea, Brenna went on the offensive. "Look, we had a thing going. It was great, then it wasn't. He's leaving. I'm staying. End of story."

"Except you're heartbroken," Andrea said.

"So is he," Penelope added.

Brenna hated the spark of hope she felt at Penelope's words. The younger woman was falling in love and was probably loved in return. She saw Cupids zipping through the air every other minute.

"How do you know?" Malina asked—the consummate investigator.

Penelope focused on Brenna's face. "It's obvious he's miserable. He used to smile all the time. He enjoyed explaining the equipment to me. He always answered all my questions."

"He isn't sleeping, either," Sloan said.

Brenna shifted her gaze in her direction. "How do you know that?"

Sloan was clearly pleased with Brenna's sharp tone. "He told me. I went down to the marina to see if I could help with anything."

"I'm not surprised he's exhausted." Looking forlorn, Penelope shook her head. "All he does is patrol, fish and lock himself in his cabin all night to do research."

"You'd think all that *leisure fishing* would relax him," Malina said drily.

Everybody found somewhere else to look.

Malina, like everyone else, certainly suspected Gavin and his crew were violating the court order, but Brenna and Gavin's crew had all been careful not to say the wrong thing, or allow her to witness anything that would compromise her duty to report her findings.

All the more reason for Gavin to lock up all the treasure until the court made its decision and leave the island ASAP.

"Did you have an argument?" Andrea asked, clearly hoping to divert the conversation from the volatile subject of "fishing" expeditions.

"Not a specific one," Brenna said. "We disagree about a lot of things."

Sloan raised her eyebrows. "You always seemed compatible when I saw you together."

"That's physical." Brenna angled her head. "Or maybe chemical. We never had any trouble there. It's everything else that's a problem."

"Like?" Andrea prompted.

Somehow Brenna didn't think the nuances of Lincoln and the Gettysburg Address were the direction to go. "*The Carolina*'s recovery is at the top of the list," she said, hoping to explain in terms she could quantify. "His goals are true, but his methods and motivations are skewed. I respect the work he does. He's literally saving history, piece by piece, but—"

"So we've noticed." Looking amused, Sloan buttered a roll the waitress had brought. "He's come a long way from being a moneygrubbing, morally vacant opportunist, wouldn't you say?"

Brenna pursed her lips. "At this point, I'd like to add that you two—" she pointed at Sloan and Andrea "—were the ones who pushed me into bed with him in the first place."

"And apparently there was some really intense pillow talk in between all that chemistry." Sloan grinned. "Like to share?"

"Excuse me." Andrea raised her finger. "We didn't push you two into bed. We nudged you. The rest was all your doing."

Sloan's bright blue eyes danced. "Both chemical and physical."

"And biological," Malina added.

"We've all been there."

At these words from Penelope, everyone's head swiveled in her direction. "I do have a boyfriend," she said, her face turning a lovely shade of pink.

"I'm not blaming you guys," Brenna said, knowing Penelope didn't want a dozen questions about her and Finn launched at her. "I'm *sharing*. And all of you already know I changed my mind about Gavin's qualifications and intent weeks ago."

She cast a cautious glance at Malina. It was possible the agent knew Gavin's true identity. But she couldn't say anything, any more than Brenna could.

"But I don't like how he's reacted to Loff coming here," Brenna continued. "He wants to win at all costs."

"We all want Loff off the island," Sloan said, ever practical.

"And Dr. Fortune's doing more than anyone to protect the treasure," Penelope said.

"Yeah. One more victory for the great Gavin Fortune," Brenna said heatedly. "The grave's dug. The only things left are remnants of lives lost."

Andrea's eyes reflected her support and sympathy. "Honey, this isn't your great-grandmother. This isn't personal."

"Sure it is," Sloan argued. "This is our history."

"I don't like what this is doing to Brenna," Andrea returned.

"Neither do I," Sloan agreed. "But the artifacts Fortune has found are important to the entire island. Brenna understands that more than any of us."

Tears filled Penelope's eyes. "She's sacrificing her relationship with the man she loves for us."

"You people are crazy," Malina said before Brenna could protest. "Brenna didn't break up with him because of the treasure or Loff or some rotting-on-the-bottom-of-the-ocean pirate ship. He's leaving. She's staying. That can only mean one thing."

Brenna swallowed hard. If anybody could cut through the bull to the truth it was Malina. Brenna braced herself for the humiliation, to hear the words aloud.

Malina didn't disappoint.

"He wants to be a treasure hunter more than he wants to be with you," she said.

Somehow relieved, Brenna nodded.

As the other women protested and sympathized, the way only women can do, Brenna reflected on the last few weeks.

She'd dreamed too intently.

His golden eyes and beautiful body had attracted her, but with his words and his passion for history, she'd been truly seduced. Maybe she should have known better. She'd been involved in an intense relationship once before, with a man who'd made promises he couldn't keep.

Gavin hadn't bothered to make promises at all.

Was that better or worse?

In the end, she hadn't expected more than the moment, and that's what she'd gotten.

Janey brought their meals, but Brenna couldn't even find comfort in Mabel's wonderful cooking.

"We can pull out," Sloan said, her blue eyes full of feeling as she gazed at Brenna.

Brenna jerked herself from regrets that wouldn't change anything. "Pull out?"

Sloan casually pushed her fork through a mound of mashed potatoes and gravy, but no one mistook her movements for nonchalance. "Pull our support for Fortune's crew. Call off the surveillance. Convince Sister Mary Katherine he's a creep."

Petty, right?

Sure. But Brenna had no doubt Sloan would offer to help bury Gavin's body along with the lost crew of *The Carolina* if she wanted.

In some ways she wanted him to hurt as much as she hurt, but she simply couldn't. That's what Loff would do. Somebody had to stop the cycle of vindictiveness and self-centeredness.

Not to mention planning a murder with an FBI agent present was probably not a good idea.

Brenna shook her head. "I want him to have the treasure. He'll make sure it's treated with respect and gets into the right hands." She set down the fork she wasn't using as an idea came to her. "In fact, Sloan, I think you should talk to Aidan right away about a new project we're going to launch."

"He needs a new one," Sloan said, looking intrigued. "He's running out of rooms at our house to remodel. What did you have in mind?"

Excitement rushed down Brenna's spine.

Here was a way to turn her time with Gavin into something lasting. Something that mattered. And she'd gotten the idea from that snake Dan Loff.

They had all the tools—Andrea's appraisal expertise, plus her husband's position as sheriff and connection to the town council clearing the way for permits. Sloan could be in charge of historical research and garner island support. Malina could handle security, with former criminal Finn as consultant. Carr in charge of legal issues; Aidan in charge of building and fundraising. Penelope could keep them organized.

Andrea nudged Brenna. "So what's the idea?"

Brenna's gaze swept her friends, the very strength and future of the island, and smiled. "We're going to establish a memorial museum for the victims of *The Carolina*."

"We are?" Andrea asked.

"How?" Malina asked.

"We'll manage," Penelope answered, grinning from ear to ear.

Sloan stared at Brenna, then nodded. "We certainly will."

"GET YOUR ASS UP."

Lying on the sofa in his boat's cabin, Gavin glanced at the doorway, where Pablo stood. His arms were crossed over his chest, and he had an expression on his face that promised serious confrontation.

Even if his words hadn't been a major clue.

Deliberately, Gavin shifted his gaze back to his book. "I'm researching the *Star of Ariana.*"

"By now, I'd imagine you know everything about every star in the universe."

"Impossible."

"Well, then, you're pretty versed in avoidance."

Casually, Gavin turned a page he hadn't read. "If people wouldn't bother me, I wouldn't have to avoid them."

"It's not as fun following Loff every step he takes unless you're there. He gets all red in the face and sputters like he's forgotten how to talk whenever he sees you."

"Sorry I'm spoiling the merriment."

"You're the face of this organization. Everybody at Joe's is asking for you. You do PR, not me. *You* schmooze the locals."

"Do I?"

"Sure. I'm the brains."

This, as was intended, got Gavin's attention. "In your dreams, man."

"You can't get the girl and the accolades, too."

"You're not me, but you're certainly smart enough to realize I don't have the girl anymore."

"Why?"

"Because I have to find the *Star of Ariana.*"

"Why?"

Gavin had no reasonable answer. "It's my job" was starting to sound ridiculous, even to him.

Pablo moved closer. He knelt next to the sofa. "Are you listening to yourself?"

The guilt and loneliness in his heart threatened to jump out. "Not if I can help it."

"Great. Listen to me."

Gavin had walked right into that one. "Fine." Jerking to his feet, he slammed the book closed and tossed it behind him on the couch. "Let's have it."

As Pablo rose, his dark eyes burned in a way Gavin had never seen them do except when they'd uncovered a treasure so amazing, words weren't necessary. "You're striving for a legacy you've already got. You're fighting an enemy you've already beaten."

Gavin flung his hand in the direction of the pier. "Oh, yeah? Then why is my enemy cooling his heels less than fifty feet away, just waiting for an opportunity to steal *my* treasure?"

Pablo shook his head. "The islanders won't let that happen. I don't know how you've done it, but they'll fight to the death for you."

"I didn't do it," Gavin said with a sigh. "Brenna did."

"Did she?" Pablo queried in a surprised tone that fooled neither of them. "She must have seen something in you that caused her to trust you with her island's history."

"I don't know what. She hates Gavin Fortune."

Pablo said nothing for a long while. "You do know you just talked about yourself in the third person."

With a laugh bordering on despair, Gavin sank to the sofa. "Brenna hated that, too."

"You are Gavin Fortune," Pablo added slowly, as if uncertain about Gavin's sanity.

Which, face it, wasn't too far off the mark.

Without Brenna, the light was gone from his life. "Am I?" he asked, glancing up at his best friend.

"Uh, buddy…"

Gavin waved off Pablo's worried expression. "I mean, metaphorically. In my drive to beat Loff and those like him, have I turned into them? Have I become greedy and petty? Have I decided that winning, no matter the cost or what rules I have to break, is all that matters?"

"We're protecting the treasure."

"But from who? Maybe somebody should be protecting it from us. Aren't we stopping Loff from doing the very thing we are? I'm risking my own freedom, yours, Dennis and Jim's. For what?"

"A big-ass chest of gold and jewels."

Gavin shook his head ruefully. "For a button."

The sacrifice of the lost meant as much to him as it did Brenna. Almost. He wasn't willing to lose her.

He'd earned her respect as a protector of ghosts and gems and buttons. It was time he showed her there was a man worth admiring beneath all the artifice.

"I started the whole Fortune thing to protect my family's reputation."

"And get the girls," Pablo added.

"That, too." But what had seemed necessary for so long now seemed silly. Fake. Part of the past. He was going to live his future as a man the Randalls could claim proudly. "But I don't need him anymore."

"Uh…buddy?"

"I know, I know. It won't happen again after today. I'm going to be Gavin Randall again—exclusively. And I'm through hunting treasure. I'm going to write a book."

"Glad to hear it. Is this going to help you get the girl, so you can stop moping around here like somebody died?"

As his mind whirled with possibilities, Gavin's heart jolted back to life, as if it had been sleeping for the last week and only now found a reason to start pumping again. "I hope so. No more diving."

"Okay."

He jerked to his feet once more. "I need a shower."

"Okay."

Grinding to a halt at the entrance to the hallway, he spun. "And all the keys to the storage facility."

"What for?"

"We're going to turn them over to the judge in Charleston."

Pablo sighed, but pulled his key out of his pocket and handed it over. "I'm glad you found your conscience after we've found nearly all the treasure."

Gavin winced. "It's symbolic."

"Brenna might buy that. Can I make a suggestion?"

"Sure."

"If you're losing the Fortune thing and going part time, you're going to need somebody else to take over the PR and schmooze the locals."

"Right. Who?"

A wide grin appeared on Pablo's face. "Me."

Gavin smiled back. "That's genius."

"Told you I was the smart one."

14

BRENNA AND HER FRIENDS left Mabel's and retreated to Sloan's and Aidan's place, which was mere blocks away.

Since the house was part of the island's history, having been built in the early 1800s and lovingly restored by her friends over the last year, the historical setting spurred ideas, and the primo snacks and wine cellar only added to the party. Most of the guys had joined them as well, except for Carr, who was still in Chicago.

And though Brenna was the odd one out, she didn't feel alone. Finding Gavin, then losing him had shown her that life's happiness could be fleeting, and she needed to grab every fulfilling minute she could.

Seated at the stunning antique dining table, surrounded by people who loved her, she was doing okay.

"So, I guess we have plenty of property options for the museum, then," Sloan said drily as her husband completed reciting his list of real estate they owned—which had taken a good ten minutes.

Aidan kissed his wife's temple. "Between us and Carr, I think we'll find a suitable spot."

Malina toasted Sloan with her wineglass. "I think it's pretty damn hilarious you don't even know what your husband owns."

"Oh?" Sloan blinked in mock surprise. "So you know everything about Carr's real estate investments, do you?"

"He's not my husband," Malina pointed out.

"And when are you two going to correct that minor oversight?" Andrea, who'd married Tyler this past winter and was an expert art appraiser, gave Malina an appraising look.

Clearly wishing she'd never opened her mouth, Malina muttered, "Eventually. Don't rush me."

From across the table, Tyler dipped a chip in salsa. "Does anybody else get the feeling she says that to Carr about once a week?"

Brenna laughed, and even if she sounded rusty, it felt good. "Carr will win her over eventually."

Malina pointed her finger at Brenna. "Hey, I'm not a prize to be—"

"Since we're clearly going to be waiting awhile on Malina and Carr…" Andrea interrupted, her gaze going to her brother and Penelope, who were sitting at the end of the table.

While the implications of Andrea's words were still resonating, Penelope stood, a shaky but pleased smile on her face. "I wasn't sure I should say anything. You know, given the circumstances…" She glanced at Brenna. "But Andrea said it was okay, so, well…we're engaged."

As Brenna's jaw dropped, Penelope held out her left hand, where a diamond solitaire sparkled on her ring finger.

Everyone rushed the young couple at once.

As Brenna got her turn to embrace Penelope, she asked, "When did this happen?"

"A few days ago," her friend said, looking worried. "The day you and Dr. Fortune, well…split."

Brenna hugged her again. "You didn't have to wait to tell everybody because of me."

"We had to tell Andrea and Tyler first, anyway." Her voice was thick with emotion. "I still believe in Dr. Fortune," she added in a whisper.

Brenna smiled, not wanting to dampen her friend's optimism.

As they were all examining the ring and finding out the engagement was going to be a long one—Penelope wanted to finish school before marrying—the doorbell rang.

"I'll get it," Andrea volunteered.

Because Brenna knew Malina missed her man, she hoped Carr had guessed where they all were. If Carr had good news, plans for the museum could be brainstormed along with an engagement party.

Aidan apparently had the same idea, for he headed out of the room in search of champagne.

The celebration quieted, though, when they all clearly heard Andrea's raised voice from the direction of the foyer. "...got a lot of nerve coming here now, Fortune."

Brenna's breath caught. Gavin?

After a pause, Andrea shouted, "Yes, she's here! But you can't—"

A second later, as Brenna's pulse took flight, Gavin appeared in the dining room doorway.

"Brenna?" he asked in shock, his gaze finding her among the crowd around Penelope and Finn.

"If you would have let me finish," Andrea said, rushing in behind him, "I could have told you Brenna is here, too."

"Too?" Sloan frowned. "You're not here to see Brenna?"

"I came to see Agent Blair," Gavin said, though his gaze never budged from Brenna's.

Had he always been that beautiful? Brenna wondered. Wearing long loose shorts and a T-shirt, with his hair tied back, he looked like the scoundrel she'd first encountered weeks ago.

Her throat closed at the thought that this might be the last image she'd have of him.

"I mean, I—" Gavin cleared his own throat. "I was coming to her next, but I needed to do something first."

While everybody stared at him in startled silence, Malina

crossed her arms over her chest and suddenly looked every inch a cop. "You need the FBI, Dr. Fortune?"

Gavin finally dragged his attention to the agent. "Sort of. Judge Michaelson left town to spend the weekend at his beach house, and I wanted to hand these over to a federal official right away." Approaching Malina, he dropped a set of small keys into her palm. "They unlock the storage unit holding all the artifacts from *The Carolina*'s wreck site."

Seeing them, Brenna had known exactly what they were before he'd explained.

He was leaving.

Unfortunately, she didn't feel relief. She was devastated.

"Could I talk to you alone for a minute?"

Blinking back tears, Brenna looked up to find him directly in front of her. "I—"

"No." Sloan stepped between them before Brenna could find her voice. "You've caused enough heartache around here. I'd like you to leave."

"Give him a chance," Tyler said, drawing Sloan away. "Look at him."

As Sloan apparently followed this directive, Brenna did the same. The flecks of gold in his eyes were bright, full of…well, something that hadn't been there before. More than passion. And certainly not the regret of goodbye.

"The back porch light's on," Sloan said finally.

Brenna let Gavin slip his hand around hers and lead her out of the room and through the kitchen. They'd shared their first kiss on this deck, a mere three weeks ago, she realized with a jolt.

The beginning and the end?

"I'm through exploring *The Carolina*," he said before she could piece through the events and figure out what his appearance really meant. "I won't go back there until the courts work out its proper owner."

"Convenient, now that you've recovered all the treasure."

To her surprise, he smiled. "You and Pablo are really in sync today."

Before she could figure out what that cryptic statement was about, he continued, "You were right, and I was wrong. I wanted to beat Loff, and I didn't care how I went about it. But I care what you think about me, and I couldn't live with myself, knowing I was disappointing you."

Brenna searched his gaze. "You stopped the hunt because of me?"

He took both her hands in his. "There's nothing I wouldn't do for you. Malina can hand over the keys to the judge, and I won't touch the treasure unless the court rules in favor of Sea Oats Shipping."

"So you are leaving."

"No. Well...yes. Sort of." When he laughed uncomfortably, she realized he was nervous. But Gavin Fortune and butterflies didn't go together. "I still have to find the *Star of Ariana*. But I want you to come with me."

Certain she'd been hallucinating, Brenna shook her head to clear it. "Huh?"

He cupped her cheek in his hand and leaned down so they were eye to eye. "I love you. I want you with me—forever. I don't want a temporary hookup. I want a future with you, and I'd like to start right away."

At each word, Brenna's heart leaped a little higher, until she was sure it was spinning out the top of her head. She wrapped her arms around him and kissed him with all the pent-up fear and despair she'd been drowning in since she'd left him.

The warmth of his body and his lips enveloped her until the pain and cold were only a memory.

"Is that a yes?" he asked when she pulled back to catch her breath.

"Yes. I love you. I'll go wherever you want."

He hugged her against his chest, lifting her off her feet. "I'm going to need a new first mate. But the trip to London will be short. After we find the *Star,* I'm retiring from treasure hunting. Here." He pointed at the deck beneath his feet.

"On Palmer's Island? Why here?"

His grin was wide and perfect. "Because you're here, of course. I think I'll write a book."

"About *The Carolina?*"

"No, something boring and academic. I might get around to writing my memoirs eventually."

Still reeling from the wild turn her life had taken in the last few minutes, she smiled shyly. "Would you consider writing a book about the ship sooner?"

He seemed to sense the question wasn't random. "If you think I should."

She really liked his obvious need to please her. The gloom of his eventual departure, signaling the end of them, was gone, and in its place was a shimmering hope with all the depth of the oceans he so loved exploring.

Though, she admitted silently, she hoped she could convince him to go into *semi*retirement. She might enjoy a fling with Gavin Fortune every summer.

She explained about the museum, and he agreed a book about the hunt would be a great way to kick off publicity for the grand opening.

"The name Gavin Fortune could really bring some attention to the project," she concluded.

He suddenly looked hesitant. "Ah, well, we might have a problem there."

"Why's that?"

"I'll explain in a minute." He handed her a box. "First, this."

It was obviously from a jeweler, but bigger than a ring box. For which she was grateful. Everything was already moving so fast. After the whirlwind of the last few weeks, maybe they should slow down a bit.

Still, she opened the box with anticipation fluttering in her stomach. It wasn't an engagement ring. It was better.

Lying against the dark blue velvet was her grandmother's broach.

"It's not the actual one," Gavin said quickly. "But it's an exact duplicate."

Breathless, she lifted her gaze to his. "How? When?"

"I'm a highly trained researcher, you know." He pressed a brief kiss to her lips. "I had a friend of mine make it after you told me about your family's loss. I've had it awhile. I was going to give it to you when I left."

She traced the creamy pearls with her fingertip. "A parting gift?"

"How about a new beginning gift instead?"

"Okay."

She angled her head for another kiss, this one longer and filled with tender promise. He was a man who respected the past, but cared more about the future. And he was all hers.

"To be continued," he said softly, "for now…" He grasped her hand and led her back inside.

The crowd was gathered around the dining room table. And though filled champagne glasses sat in front of each person, they didn't appear to have been drunk from. No one—with the exception Penelope, judging from the confident expression on her face—seemed to be in a mood to celebrate.

Brenna experienced a second of regret that she'd spoiled the celebratory toast for her friend and Finn. But maybe now they could all toast to more than one couple's happy future.

"Well?" Sloan prompted when Brenna just stood there, grinning like an idiot.

"We're both leaving briefly," Brenna said, knowing her friends would understand, "then we're both staying permanently."

Everyone rushed them as they'd done to Penelope and Finn only minutes before. Gavin was welcomed into the fold as if none of them had ever threatened him—or called him a moneygrubbing, morally vacant opportunist.

"This calls for a double toast," Aidan said, passing glasses to Gavin and Brenna, then filling them with champagne.

"I knew you'd come through, Dr. Fortune," Penelope said as the clink of crystal sang through the air.

"Don't you think it's time you call him Gavin?" Brenna suggested to her friend.

"I agree." Gavin cleared his throat. "Especially since my name's not really Fortune."

Brenna choked on her champagne. "What're you doing?"

He stroked her cheek with the pad of his thumb. "Earning your respect." To the group, he said, "Fortune is a pseudonym I've been using for treasure hunting. My real last name is Randall."

"You knew this, Brenna?" Andrea asked.

She nodded. "I did."

"That's what convinced you of his sincerity about protecting *The Carolina*," Finn concluded.

Brenna exchanged a loving look with Gavin. "It was a bit more involved than that, but, yes, it was a start."

"Are you really from Austin?" Penelope asked.

Gavin assured her he was.

"Hang on. Texas?" Sloan's stunned eyes focused on Gavin. "As in the Randall Foundation?"

"My great-grandfather started it. Now my parents run everything."

There was a lengthy silence as everyone tried to adjust to the knowledge that the supposedly shallow adventurer was actually part of one of the most wealthy, respected and philanthropic families in the country. Then Malina toasted him. "Great. You make the first donation to the museum."

Gavin nodded. "Glad to."

This sudden change of fortune got the room buzzing with excitement yet again.

Brenna wrapped her arm around his waist. "So the first book by Gavin Randall will be about *The Carolina?*"

"Fitting, don't you think?"

"Definitely." She melted into the gold of his eyes. "But you didn't have to do that. I'm proud to be by your side no matter what your name is."

He kissed her. "Thank you, but it was time."

"Who's going to take over treasure hunting?"

"Pablo. We'll have to come up with a cool, new name for him."

"What's the Spanish word for fortune?"

"I think it's something similar, like *fortuna*. But that's a great place to start. He's looking forward to balancing his work with being a professional, good-natured lothario."

"We can't let the bikini-clad babes of the world get lonely."

"True, they'll have to survive without me. But I'll be sure to give Pablo tips from time to time. I can't have my partner embarrassing the family."

"As long as you explain, not demonstrate."

Leaning his face close to hers, he grinned. "Deal. You can—"

"I got it."

At Carr's announcement, everybody turned toward the doorway. Obviously, they'd all been too wrapped up in the night's revelations to hear his arrival.

"When did you get back?" Malina asked, moving toward her boyfriend and embracing him.

"Just now." Carr kissed Malina and spoke quietly to her before focusing on the others. "Loff's sunk."

"How?" Brenna asked, moving toward him with Gavin at her side.

Carr handed her a stack of papers. "The evidence of Loff's ownership of *The Carolina*. Check out the highlighted area on page seven."

With Gavin looking over her shoulder, Brenna flipped to that page and found what appeared to be a copy of an old bill of sale from the Sea Oats Shipping Company to Captain James

Cullen. So far, nothing looked like cause for the happiness so clearly stamped on Carr's face.

Until she got to the highlighted portion, which was the date of the sale. The first day of August, 1885.

"1885?" Gavin echoed in disbelief. "The Union Army sank the ship in 1863."

Looking highly pleased with himself, Carr rocked back on his heels. "Exactly. We assume the date was meant to be 1858. The judge's clerk and I figured Loff was in such a hurry to make up his fake documents, he transposed the eight and the five. It's correct in the transcript of court statements and in other places in the paperwork. But since this document is a supposed photocopy of the actual bill of sale held by Captain Cullen, it looks like exactly what it is. A scam."

Brenna's hands shook as she handed the paper to Penelope, so she could see the evidence for herself. This whole business was beginning to sink in. They had proof of Loff's fraud.

Something she'd bet Gavin's whole family portfolio the federal government wouldn't look fondly upon.

From behind her, Gavin squeezed her shoulders. He'd apparently grasped the implications, as well.

"The family tree's fiction, too," Carr said, slipping off his suit coat and hanging it over the back of a chair. "I don't have proof of that yet, except the clerk's word."

"How did the judge miss such an important detail?" Sloan asked as she, too, stared in disbelief at the documents.

Carr's dark eyes sparkled. "Here's where the news gets better."

Aidan raised his eyebrows. "Better? Surely those tiny but important numbers make everything fairly straightforward."

"I bet you'd like to hear about the twists and turns." Carr rolled up the sleeves of his dress shirt, as if the story up till now had only been a warm-up. "So, I used my charm and guile on Judge Donner's court clerk."

"Was this a female clerk, by any chance?" Brenna asked.

The darkly handsome attorney made quite an impression in the courtroom and anywhere else he went.

Carr looked insulted. "As a matter of fact, no."

"So you threatened him," Malina said smartly.

Carr waved a hand. "Only a little. This is Chicago, after all. I'd imagine the court has seen more intimidating characters than me. Anyway, after half a beer, the guy cracked and blubbered the whole story all over me. I had to promise to represent him if there's a misconduct hearing."

Malina linked hands with him. "Softy," she teased, though she seemed proud.

"And I imagine there will be an investigation, possibly leading to disbarment, since Judge Donner apparently didn't look too hard at the bill of sale, because Loff is blackmailing him."

"Huh?" everyone seemed to ask at once.

"It seems Loff sold Donner a piece from a shipwreck several years back," Carr continued. "But the salvage contents actually belonged to the French government, who'd commissioned Loff and his team to find the ship. Loff was supposed to catalog the artifacts and get a monetary percentage of the sales."

Gavin sighed. "But he didn't catalog everything."

"Clearly not," Carr said. "Unfortunately for Judge Donner, Loff had videotaped their illicit, completely illegal exchange. Jason and I—"

"Jason?" Brenna asked.

"The clerk," Carr clarified. "Jason and I think the scheme is something Loff must do on a regular basis. I mean, what are the odds he happened to record this transaction among all the others, and this is the one we stumble onto?"

Malina's smile was cynical. "Very, very long."

"So Loff forces the judge to sign the injunction to stop Gavin's team, and neither is willing to rat out the other, because they're both crooked and guilty." Brenna shook her head. "How did clerk Jason find out?"

"Loff had warned him we'd fight the injunction," Carr said. "The judge had to get rid of Loff's documents—at least temporarily. But he didn't want them to disappear forever, so he entrusted them to his organized but pretty wimpy clerk, Jason."

"If the scheme was discovered," Tyler murmured, "they'd all be complicit."

Carr nodded. "That seems to be the most logical conclusion."

"Well, I say, hurrah for poor Jason," Andrea said. "He's the only one who was thinking."

Sloan nodded. "Or operating with any conscience."

"Except we don't know why Loff would go to so much trouble." Gavin sounded confused.

"Probably because he's desperate. It seems Loff's broke, on the verge of filing bankruptcy." At the collective gasp that followed his announcement, Carr bowed. "I told you it got better."

"The rejected credit card," Tyler mused, turning to Finn and Penelope.

"You mean flirty Tammy helped crack this case?" Brenna asked in annoyed disbelief.

Gavin brushed his lips across her chcck. "Look at it this way, my love—the entire island made this happen." His gaze swept the group. "I owe all of you a great deal. Thank you."

Andrea smiled. "Oh, you already agreed to pay, remember?"

With a laugh, Gavin pulled Brenna tight into his embrace. "So I did."

As his heart pounded against her ear, Brenna knew this was one of those fulfilling moments to cherish and appreciate. Her friends surrounding her, the love of her life tucking her securely in his arms. Life didn't get much better on Palmer's Island.

She breathed in Gavin's familiar scent and turned her face up to his. His gaze, full of love and hope, met hers. The irresistible lure she'd felt from their first meeting was as strong as ever.

Maybe life could get even better....

Carr, caught up in his dramatic news, seemed to only now notice the closeness between Gavin and Brenna, as well as the food and champagne. "You guys celebrating? What'd I miss?"

As everyone else laughed, Malina patted him sympathetically on the chest.

Meanwhile, Aidan headed toward the kitchen, presumably to get yet another champagne glass. "At this rate, everybody's going to be toasted by the time the night's out."

Epilogue

"Babe, have you seen my white dress shirt?" Gavin called, tossing a stack of travel magazines off the bed.

"Did you try the closet?" Brenna called from the bathroom.

Gavin scanned the bedroom, which was cluttered with stacks of boxes and furniture still covered in plastic. "I'd need a GPS to find the closet. Who's stuff is all this, anyway?"

Brenna poked her head around the doorway. Her strawberry-blond hair was captured in several dozen rollers, and she held a mascara wand. She looked adorable. His Irish pixie. "I think you'll notice a lot of these boxes are marked *books,* and, therefore, yours."

"Then they should be downstairs in my office."

"Nothing is where it's supposed to be," Brenna reminded him. "*Somebody*—again, you come to mind—was in a big hurry to christen the new bed in the new house last night and told the movers to drop the boxes anywhere they wanted."

Unrepentant, Gavin grinned. "It *is* a great house."

"And, thankfully, a sturdy bed."

With fall weather finally breaking through Palmer's Island's summer heat, they'd raised the windows facing the ocean. As he picked his way across the room toward her, a brisk breeze followed him.

Her eyes bright with desire, Brenna trailed the tip of her

finger down his bare chest. "You should go to the town council meeting like this. They'll give us whatever we want."

He captured her hand, her left, kissed the emerald and diamond engagement ring, the gems of which once had been part of Captain Cullen's famed booty, then drew her against him.

She'd belonged to him from the first moment he'd seen her. Now, everyone else would know it, too. "The official vote for approval is only a formality. *The Carolina* Memorial Museum is going to be the crowning jewel of the historical society. And the island."

"Director McGary," Brenna said with obvious pleasure. "I like the sound of it."

"It'll be Director Randall by the time we open the doors next year."

She pressed her lips to the base of his throat, the highest point she could reach. "So it will."

Gavin had bought a large portion of the ship's artifacts from the Sea Oats Shipping Company. A few items had been sent to descendants of the men lost and some to respected collectors, who'd donated their property to museums throughout the South.

The valuable gems and gold pieces from Cullen's treasure were sold during a splashy auction to people all over the world, with Gavin buying some of the emeralds and diamonds for Brenna's ring. She swore she didn't need the extravagance, though she wore the symbol of their commitment to each other with pride.

When he gave her the matching necklace on their wedding day, she was either going to be thrilled or embarrassed by the largesse.

He'd also purchased a few rubies, which would be hidden among the simulated gold coins and jewelry, along with Cullen's actual chest, that would all be part of the museum's permanent collection.

Watching the visitors try to guess what was real and what

wasn't would no doubt be as satisfying as seeing everything of historical significance revealed to those seeking knowledge of the island's past. The wreckage of the ship itself they'd left as an underwater monument to the crew's sacrifice.

Brenna had been unanimously elected by the society to run the museum, and though the high school was sorry to lose her, she'd promised to stay on the list of substitute teachers.

Between personal and professional plans for the future, they'd also found the *Star of Ariana,* with Brenna acting as his very own Dr. Watson by recording every step of their adventure. A story for the kids and maybe the rest of the world as his book about *The Carolina*'s discovery was coming along well.

"Think Stanley will vote against us?" she wondered.

Since Loff's check for his big party in the town square had bounced, the mayor had to bill the city to pay for the event. Somehow, in between sips of brandy, and since Loff wasn't around to rail against—he was in jail on suspicion of fraud and bribing a federal official—a desperate Stanley had managed to blame Gavin for the whole mess.

"He's probably forgiven me by now," Gavin said, resuming his search for a shirt.

"I don't know. At Mabel's yesterday, I heard people talk about needing new leadership in the mayor's office. A lifetime politician who's cornered is a dangerous animal."

The mention of animals had his gaze darting to Shakespeare Fuzzyboots, who sat curled on Brenna's pillow. His haughty expression clearly communicated he hadn't decided whether or not he liked his new home.

As a result, he was sitting on the shirt.

Gavin flung his hand toward the window and the shoreline beyond. "If that's not the world best sandbox, I don't know what is."

Obligingly, Shakes rose, and Gavin snatched the shirt, shoving his arms into the sleeves.

"Stanley's not so bad," he said to Brenna, "and he's extremely repentant about the party incident."

"How do you know that?"

The suspicion in her voice caused him to wince. "I saw him the other day, you know, just in passing on the street."

Brenna grabbed him by the loop of his pants and tugged him around to face her. "You gave him the money to pay for it, didn't you?"

"Ah…"

"Did you?"

Defeated in the face of those fierce green eyes, he nodded.

She threw her arms around his waist and hugged him tight. "I love you."

The precious words still made his heart jump. Her happiness was his new adventure, as deep as the sea and strong as the surf. The culmination of his life's work. Revenge and retaliation were no longer important. The satisfaction of defeating a rival barely significant.

His family mantra had always been service and generosity, and, with the love of his life beside him, he finally felt worthy of the legacy.

He lifted her off her feet and laid her on the brand-new mattress. Hovering over her, he drew the pad of his thumb across her smiling lips.

He hoped Stanley had forgiven him, since they were going to be really late to the meeting.

* * * * *

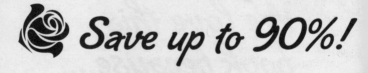